Through Her Eyes

A Novel by

Keshia LaVett

ISBN: (Paperback) - 979-8-218-18340-0

Any references to historical events, real people, or real places are used fictitiously. Names, characters, and places are products of the author's imagination.

Front cover image by sambu_arts.

Epilogue was written by Major Craig Crowley, U.S. Marine Corp.

First printing edition 2023.

Perigon Publishing

700 Rock Quarry Road

Stockbridge, GA 30281

perigonpublishing@gmail.com

Thank you, God, for a talent not hidden.

My mother, for so much love and support and most importantly, for introducing me to stories.

My daughters Angenae' and Priscilla for being the wind beneath my wings

My family and friends for your overabundance of encouragement and inspiration.

Professor Elaine Upton for always celebrating my written words.

"A special thank you to the late, legendary Walter Dean Myers for recognizing my potential!"

TABLE OF CONTENTS

CHAPTER ONE

"Stories"

"Storytelling, you know, has a real function. The process of storytelling is itself a healing process, partly because you have someone there who is taking the time to tell you a story that has great meaning to them. They're taking the time to do this because your life could use some help, but they don't want to come over and just give advice. They want to give it to you in a form that becomes inseparable from your whole self. That's what stories do. Stories differ from advice in that, once you get them, they become a fabric of your whole soul. That is why they heal you."

Alice Walker

She smelled of cooked cinnamon, perfume, freshly baked rolls, sweet potatoes, collard greens, and vinegar, all rolled up into one melody. I sat on my mother's lap with 100 pounds of skin and bone. I laid my head gently on her shoulder. Her fuzzy hair tickled my nose, but I didn't mind. There she sat, never uttering a word of discomfort, although I'm sure holding me felt like a duffle bag full of dismantled skeletons. My name is Alexandra Hope Nielson. My family and friends called me Hope, and Daddy nicknamed me Moon. I was the only girl in a family of five. My sight was always a challenge, but everything else worked just fine.

It was always nice to be so close to Momma, trying desperately to visualize the images of her tales. I felt protected, safe, loved, and captivated all at once. Her stories inspired me to become a writer. I just wished that writer's-block didn't hold my words hostage. There was nothing worse than having so many verbs, nouns, and adjectives trapped inside you, struggling to throw themselves on a blank page. No matter how hard I tried, I produced nothing. I knew I would never be as great a storyteller as Momma. She reminded me of the narrator in the introduction of Charles Dickens, *A Christmas Carol.* Her stories had mystery and humor - a great combination. When it was something funny, she imitated the characters' voices almost exactly how they spoke. She captured the low baritone pitches of the males and the squeaky, high-pitched voices of the female and sometimes male sopranos. She was so talented. It never failed, she always had me hunched over with laughter. I felt like I was listening to a comedy bit by Martin Lawrence. Hysterical! However, when her words transitioned to sadness, she brought me to tears.

When she got so engrossed in her monologue, a dimple would appear in her left cheek, and her voice would start cracking while signaling her eyes to fight back hesitant tears. Momma captured the essence of her stories. She owned them.

One day I crawled beside her on our couch and stared at her as best as I could. Momma was what we African-Americans called light-skinned. Her eyes were brown, at least that's what she told me. While cuddling with Momma, I felt how almond-shaped her eyes were and how her nose spreaded slightly on her cheeks. I was happy to be close to her. I laid my head on her thick forearm.

"Why are you so happy, Moon?"

"Nothing, Momma."

"Oh, you just go around smiling for no reason in the middle of the day?" I chuckled.

"No, I just love you, Momma," I answered, smelling the spray and shampoo mixture in her hair.

"I love you too, Moon."

"Momma?"

"Yes?"

"How do you tell your stories the way that you do?" She took a deep breath and stroked the front of my frizzy edges that somehow never wanted to stay stuck to my forehead the way hers did. She took a moment to think before she answered.

"I own my stories, Moon," she said.

"What do you mean?" I inquired.

"I've lived them, or I have witnessed them. You haven't lived enough yet, Moon, but you will." She stroked my hair again. "Don't worry."

I remembered the first story she ever told me. It was interwoven in me like a permanent piece of fabric stitched to my soul. It was a cold, damp night. It rained non-stop, and none of us could sleep listening to the rhythmic drips dancing on the metal bucket Daddy placed under the leaky roof. That's another reason why snuggling up with Momma was such a treat. Cozy. Warm. Our house always seemed to be cold and damp. However, It worked out well in the summer because we didn't get too hot.

Momma leaned back on the couch and pulled me closer. I was only seven then, so snuggling was easier. I was smaller. My legs were less muscular and didn't dangle so far to the floor. I could smell her Sta-Sof-Fro hair conditioner, and the subtle fragrance of her perfume tickled my nose. She smiled with a subtle grunt of reminiscence. After sliding her fingers through my hair, she took a deep breath, and began.

The windows were painted with thick spirals of fog, Momma said, *and the room spat out repeated moans and screams of my agony.* She sat up a little on the couch as if she could still feel the pain. *The bubbles of sweat rolled off my face as I listened to the commands of your father and Dr. Nostribub. "Push Pranita!" Dr. Nostribub catapulted his voice as he petitioned me to exert my body.*

"IT HURTS!" I shouted in excruciating pain.

"I know, but just one more big push," He said. Pearson stood on the side of the hospital bed and wiped the continuous stream of sweat popping from my head. I gave one last big huge grunt, and Dr. Nostribub wrapped you up in a pink polka-dotted blanket I ordered him to use upon arrival. It was a gift from your grandmother. As I started to calm myself, I scanned the room and noticed it smelled of betadine and bleach-treated surfaces. Blood stained the sheets. The IV needle attached to the back of my hand caused it to throb. There were also five extra

people in the room, three male and two female that crowded around you as you sat oblivious in a glass box.

"Pearson, is everything okay?" I inquired with grave concern. "Go. Hurry." I demanded. Your Daddy crept over to the crowd of people in white lab coats and attempted to intervene. Dr. Nostribub was a short Asian man with a mild but caring voice. He wore black horned-rimmed glasses that made him look smart yet mysterious. He was examining you while the others observed. Pearson didn't want to cause a major disturbance to draw attention away from you, so he gently pulled the coat of one of the doctors. "Excuse me, Ma'am." She looked up suddenly and nodded, gesturing for him to ask his question. "Sorry to bother you all. I appreciate what you're doing for my daughter." Pearson paused and swallowed nervously. "But is everything okay?"

CHAPTER TWO

"Say It's Not So"

"If you don't like something, change it. If you can't change it, change your attitude."

Maya Angelou

"We are concerned about the severe swelling around the eyes," said the female doctors.

"Okay, thank you, doctor. Should we be worried?"

"I'll let Dr. Nostribub answer that for you." She walked away toward the congregation of doctors near the entryway. They all looked like they were glowing because of the bright lights reflecting from the hallway, or maybe it was the anesthesia. Momma chuckled a little, then continued. *Dr. Nostribub kept examining your eyes with a round instrument with a black handle. He looked disturbed and curious. He thought for a little, looking straight ahead away from your father and me, but I could hear the doctors faintly.*

"For now, we will put this ointment around her eyelids daily while she's here, and I will send some home with Mr. and Mrs. Nielsen," He stated firmly."

"Yes, doctor." the nurse replied. She immediately started applying the ointment to your eyes. She re-swaddled you in the *pink polka-dotted blanket and handed you to me with your father looking on with joy, excitement, and concern.*

"What should we name her, Pranita?" Fighting back the tears that clouded my eyes, I smiled and said, "Let's name her Alexandra Hope." Your father smiled and breathed a breath of agreement.

Soon, the nurse returned to the room to take you for more blood tests and rolled you away. My heart paused and became paralyzed. I finally released the tears I had been holding back. "What's wrong with our baby girl, Pearson?" Your father always moved and spoke slowly. He turned to face me as if it pained him to turn his dark brown neck. He looked into my eyes and hesitated before speaking.

"They're concerned about her eyelids. They say they're swollen," He said quietly.

"SWOLLEN!" I yelled. I sat up as erect as I could with a grunt here and there, trying to overcome the pain from labor and delivery. "Why? Ouch!"

I grunted again in agony. "Do they know why?"

"They didn't say," he sighed with exhaustion.

Dr. Nostribub came in soon after and explained that the swollen eyelids could signify a vision problem.

"So, you mean she may be blind?" I exclaimed. He looked at me and didn't give me an answer to my question. He told us to take the eye ointment home and apply it daily.

"Okay, I will, doctor." I moaned while shifting my body to sit up straighter. "Are you saying my daughter could be blind?" I asked again with strong concern.

"It's a possibility, Ma'am" Dr. Nostribub straightened his glasses and cleared his throat, and rested his hand on the rectangular tray-like table that sat in front of the hospital bed. "We will know more once the swelling subsides and we can examine the pupils better. The pupils of both eyes should work together and over the next few months, they should follow objects you put in front of her. Pay close attention to that." He walked out of the room, allowing the heavy wooden door to slowly close tightly. I placed my head on Pearson's thin shoulder and cried. "Is this my fault?"

"No. Sometimes things just happen," Pearson said. He sat on the bed cautiously and hugged me. "We can do this as long as we're together. Our baby girl will be just fine. You watch. She's a Nielson," he declared.

Three months later, I started hearing words like acuity, vision loss, and legal blindness.

My Mom nudged me to get my attention. I looked up at her and faced her light brown eyes as they fluttered with nostalgia and sobriety. "I'm glad I named you Alexandra Hope," she said, squinching her nose while using her thumb and pointer finger to grasp my chin while gently shaking it side to side as if I were still one year old.

"Hope for short, remember that," I said.

"Yes, I remember. You were just a tiny little thing but possessed such courage, intelligence, and resilience early on," she smiled.

When learning to crawl, you ran into walls all over the house and did not cry a lick. She continued. *You were much too young for glasses. You would crawl at a steady pace toward the wall and I think you smelled the paint before approaching it. You slowed down and put your hand up to pat and feel the wall to avoid hitting it. This technique served you well for the next two years without glasses. It's how you navigated through this four-bedroom single-story house we call home.*

CHAPTER THREE

"A Glimpse"

"My mission in life is not merely to survive, but to thrive; and to do so with some passion, some compassion, some humor, and some style."

Maya Angelou

"Alexandra!" my mother yelled. I didn't answer. I wanted to finish drawing the stick figures in my journal. It's what I did when I couldn't find words. "ALEXANDRA HOPE NEILSON! Get in here now! I know you heard me calling you with that bionic hearing of yours!" I heard Momma yelling. How many times did I have to tell her that inflated senses of the blind was a myth! I was annoyed. I placed the top on my favorite pen, shifted my heavy and thick trifocals on my face, and straightened my collection of Helen Keller biographies. I looked inquisitively at my poster of Ida B. Wells as if she had something to tell me. I got out of the white wooden desk chair, slid it back under my desk, and made my way through the long shadowy hall to the kitchen. The house had no stairs. It was a rambler like all the houses in *The Stone Community*. There were four bedrooms that spread strategically around the house, and every wall was painted a shade of some bright color. My mom was really into vibrant colors. She thought if the walls were bright it would help me navigate through the house a little better. I really appreciated the gesture but it didn't help much. My parents purchased this house once they were sure my eye disease was irreversible.

When I entered the kitchen, my mom looked at me with eyes that radiated agitation. "Alexandra, just because you're seventeen and in college now doesn't give you the right to be late for family dinner." She always called it family dinner. I guess she wanted to remind me that this was the one time we were all together during the day.

"Yes, ma'am," I said respectfully. My two little brothers, Benjamin and Bailey, looked on with smirks.

"Yes, ma'am," Benjamin grinned, mocking me and laughing hysterically with his mouth wide open, displaying the chewed-up ribs and collard greens stuck to the roof of his mouth and tongue.

"Shut up, Benjamin," I retorted. The bright lights in the kitchen made it easy to locate an empty chair and witness Benjamin being a clown as usual. My brothers were like night and day. My mother thought she was finished having kids, and then, suddenly, when I turned nine, she got pregnant with Benjamin, and then less than a year later, boom, another surprise. I think babies born so close are called Irish twins. Bailey was calm and much sweeter than Benny. That's what I called Benjamin when I liked him. Dinner was delicious. Momma was a good cook. She made barbeque spare ribs, black-eyed peas, cornbread, and collard greens - Soul Food. I was so glad I remembered my trifocals. I could see the sauce glistening on the meat like the sun bouncing off the leaves in summer. The greens were smothered in vinegar, and the cornbread smelled like biscuits and cake fresh out of the oven. We barely talked during dinner because Momma's cooking was so good. Daddy was working late as usual. My brothers were stuffing large pieces of cornbread in their mouths. They competed with each other to see who could eat the fastest. Before I could take the second bite, they screamed, "Finished, Momma!" Benny screamed first.

"No, I'm finished. Stop cheating, Benny!" Bailey retorted. They ran back to their rooms, tugging and grabbing at each other's limbs.

When my mother finished eating, she started reading the newspaper. I could make out the front-page headline. It read *The Washington Post, April 29, 1992. Four White Los Angeles Police Department Officers are Acquitted of Excessive Force Charges.* "I heard about that incident last year," I called out, startling my mother.

"Oh, you did?"

"Yea." I read on. *The four white police officers were caught on video beating an intoxicated black man excessively.* "I can't believe they got off." I said. The words started jumping in doubles on the page, so I stopped reading. I saw enough. Injustice was still a living cancer, contaminating equality. I put my head down, disgruntled. After reading that, I nibbled at my spare rib, barely wanting to eat the black-eyed peas and greens. "Momma," I called.

"Yes, Moon," she answered.

"I lost my appetite," I said somberly.

"You can't let stuff like this bother you, baby," Momma stated endearingly. "African Americans have been fighting this fight for many years. It's always been a game of tug of war-justice pulls one direction, and for a while, it looks like it has most of the rope, and then injustice pulls the rope to the other side and starts winning again." Momma sighed and placed her slender caramel hands on my cinnamon ones. "You can't let it get you down! You just can't."

That night, the house was still. I could hear my brother Bailey snoring down the hall and the occasional car speeding through our street. The crickets were chirping loudly, and the sounds of a spring night were in full effect. I made numerous attempts to fall asleep, but they were unsuccessful. Finally, I decided to get up and maneuver my way back to the kitchen. I wanted a glass of warm milk, but no one was up to make it for me. With my welcoming fluorescent light, I spotted the figment immediately lying-in wait on the kitchen table. It was the newspaper. I sat down to try and read more of the article about the four white police officers. I could barely make out the words. I left my glasses in my room on the desk. It was so frustrating. I could only make out the words not guilty and 26-year-old Rody Kin, but I was determined to read the article, so I grabbed it and felt my way back to my room, sliding my hand tentatively along the popcorn-painted walls. I desperately wanted to get to my desk, my glasses, and the article. I wished I could have sprinted down the hall without injury, but I knew that wasn't my reality, so I allowed the wall to continue to lead me like a trusted tour guide. Slowly and steadily, I made it down the hallway to my room.

Once I made it there, I immediately put on my glasses and examined the article. I looked closer at the photograph of the four white officers and realized that a barbeque smudge cut off part of the badge of one of the cops. That was good, I thought. He didn't deserve a badge, so I was glad part of it was hidden. The article spoke of the four officers' great contributions to the community. I stopped reading. I took out my journal and attempted to write. My journal was part of my arsenal. It was how I fought back. I always thought I was helpless without my sight. Who's going to listen to a black, blind female? I thought. So I spoke through the lines of my entries even though I didn't have a real audience.

Last year on my sixteenth birthday, my parents bought me my first Walkman. My vision had been a challenge ever since I discovered my senses, so my other favorite thing to do was to listen. I loved to listen to Momma's stories and her music. Well, not her music, but music from her day. The songs from the sixties and seventies. My aunt Addie always came over, and she and my Momma would sit in the kitchen for hours, eating soul food and talking about life.

My favorite memory was of the two of them listening to James Brown songs on the record player. My favorite song was "Say it Loud." This song spoke to me deeply. The lyrics carried me along with every word and note. He sang of defying injustice. He sang of America's crime of robbing black people of their pride. Pride is rooted in the great attributes that make us who we are- our hair, skin, resilience, and strength. All things to be proud of! He sang the chorus repeatedly,

"Say it loud. I'm black, and I'm proud." And I sang it right with him. I was bobbing my head and shaking my hips as I repeated the words,

"Say it loud. I'm black, and I'm proud." I made sure my aunt Addie saw me dancing. Her response always fueled my moves.

"Get it, Hope!" She would yell, smiling and clapping. Those words were still relevant in 1992. My hair was loosely curly and fine, but I always washed it and refrained from oiling it to let it dry strong because of this song. Because of this song, I yearned to do something other than write to fight, but I did nothing but write, and writer's block wouldn't even let me do that.

I placed my Walkman headphones on my ear and listened to another oldie but goodie. Marvin Gaye's *"What's Going On"* played as I laid in my bed, enveloped in soft pillows and blankets. I smiled as his voice went, *"Mother, mother. There's too many of you crying. Brother, brother, brother. There's far too many of you dying*

CHAPTER FOUR

"Me and the World"

"I can do everything through Him who gives me strength."

Philippians 4:13

"Hope! Hope! Moon, I know you hear me," screamed Momma. She knocked on the door like a policeman searching for a wanted person. I didn't hear her right away. I had on my Walkman blasting Public Enemy's Fight *the Power.* I stopped drawing stick figures in my journal, placed my pen in my desk's top drawer, and opened the door. I sighed a long, irritating sigh. "Yes, Momma."

"What in the world are you doing in here, Hope?"

"Sorry, Momma. I was wearing my Walkman."

"You and that damn Walkman," yelled Momma.

"Angel is in the living room waiting for you."

"Be there in a minute," I yelled. Angel has been my best friend since I was twelve. She lived next door and didn't mind my thick goofy glasses. Momma didn't like people wandering around the house. She was sometimes very private. I always had to go and get Angel from the living room and escort her to my room. It was good because Angel had 20/20 vision, and she would always grab my hand and hurry me to my room. It was great. It was the only time I got to my room fast from the living room. She and I looked like sisters. I was cinnamon brown with big, almond-shaped eyes and short curly hair. Angel was caramel with big, almond-shaped eyes and long curly hair. If it were the seventies, she and I would do wonders for the Afro. We had been inseparable since the seventh grade. I was always at her house. Her mom and dad made their house vision-impaired friendly, just for me.

At the doorway of Angel's room was a bright orange doormat that contrasted well with the dark hardwood floor. Angel liked the Hip Hop group TLC, so she placed a poster of their debut album, "Ooooooooohhh… On the TLC Tip," on the wall. It was full of bright colors. T-Boz, Left-Eye, and Chili wore an assortment of contrasting primary colors like bright reds and yellow, while Left-Eye sported red plaid shorts. The background included patterns of stripes and zig zags. Posters like this were strategically placed above pieces of furniture like her desk chair and bed - all places I may have sat.

The furniture in the living room was spaced out in case I needed to stretch my arms out in the dark to feel my way around, and I could without tripping or falling. Whenever I stayed for dinner, Mrs. Womack placed my canary yellow plate on a dark blue placemat and placed a yellow ring around a dark blue cloth napkin. I always knew right away which table setting was mine. It was always nice to visit. I felt like one of the family. They did a really good job of balancing giving me independence and providing me with a little support. I liked that. Mr. and Mrs. Womack made me feel like one of their kids. They had Winston,

Nicholas, Angel, and me-Hope. Yep, I was the fourth child of Winston Sr. and Carol Womack.

When Angel entered my room, she sat on my bed and looked at the news clippings and posters on my wall. She spied pictures of Ida B. Wells, Phillis Wheatley, Malcolm X, Martin Luther King, and an old 1950s Jet magazine clipping of Emmit Till's open casket at his funeral in 1955. There was also an iconic picture of Coretta Scott King looking ever so beautiful, wearing a black veil over her face sitting sadly at her husband Martin Luther King's funeral in 1968. She continued along the timeline wall and stared at a clipping of the Mississippi Burning Murders of 1964. She stopped and idled over a clipping of the 1992 verdict of the Rodney King beating. She had seen all of these pictures and clippings before except for the pictures of the four officers who were acquitted of King's videoed public beating, so I didn't know why she was staring as if it was her first time. My family did the same thing whenever they visited my room. I think it was because they were all so compelling. The clippings often made me pause. Think. Reflect. Realize.

Angel kicked the two balls of socks in the middle of the floor to the side, moved my jeans out of the way, and sat on my bed.

"Take your shoes off if you're going to stretch out," I said.

"My shoes are clean, just like my body and my pearly white teeth," she answered, leaning and shaking her head side to side with sassiness while making an irritating CHEEEEEESE sound and looking tight-faced. Her face looked like the one we made when the school photographer was taking our picture.

"Well, they better stay off of my bed." I retorted.

"Whatever, Hope Hope," Angel replied.

"What's Up? I said. Angel examined my wall again, a little closer.

"Every time I come in here, I feel like I'm stepping into a black history time capsule," she said, laughing. "You going to the campus rally tonight?" Angel inquired.

"No." I paused. "I want to, but..." I paused again. "I'm scared, Angel, shoot! Stop asking me," I retorted.

"Hope, are you ever going to leave this house without your bodyguards? Your mom still walks you one hundred yards to my house, or she makes me come and get you," Angel said with agitation.

"I don't know," I shrugged.

Angel and I attended the District of Columbia University. The difference was she went to all of her classes without an escort. I graduated from the Maryland School for the Blind a year before her. She was still attending high school while I took all of my classes at DCU. She only came to DCU to take Business Calculus. Yep, she had beauty and brains just like me. She wanted to be an accountant slash model. We used to talk about me doing a cover story about supermodel Angel Womack - written by Alexandra Nielson.

My mother was a stay-at-home mom, and my father was a tractor-trailer driver for the United States Postal Service. It paid him well. We were able to live in *The Stone Community* comfortably, although Daddy was the worst at keeping up with house repairs. The roof and heating in this house was always a challenge. It was a normal upper-middle-class neighborhood. Whatever normal meant. With my Daddy paying all the bills, my Momma had time to escort me to the two classes I took at DCU. I always took morning classes so Momma could be home in time to greet Benny and Bailey when they got home from school. She didn't sit in the lecture halls with me. She made sure I got to each class safely, and then she waited outside for an hour for the class to be over. I carried a symbol stick. That's a cane the blind or partially sighted people used as a flag or symbol to let fully sighted people know they had a vision impairment. It was obviously used to help the vision impaired navigate their surroundings, but secretly the stick also prompted people to offer their assistance whenever I was in need; most of the time they did. Momma or my brothers were usually not far from me when I was out in public, but sometimes, like when I was in class, I could use a little help to get seated or with my backpack, so the stick came in handy. I paused, looked at my Helen Keller biographies, and said nothing.

"I'm just saying, Hope, you're seventeen." Angel sat up on my bed and continued,

"You've never kissed a boy, been on a real date, or been to a party. I know you don't enjoy the mall, but even if you did, you would never go without your mother. You can't keep living like this," she declared.

My eyes were blurred, but not because of my vision. It was the tears swelling up around my eyeballs like unwanted invaders. All of a sudden, Angel stopped talking. She observed my overactive tear ducts and got up to console me. During our silent embrace, the same questions that had lived in my head for the last year were awakened. What guy would want me in these goggles? What sexy party outfit would go with these goggles? How would I get around an unfamiliar place without looking handicapped? How many people would stare at me in my discomfort? How would I mingle when I could barely see the people I'm mingling with? I aggressively removed myself from Angel's embrace, wiped my tears with my fingertips and some with my palms, and sat at my desk drinking the cup of Hawaiian Punch my Mom brought in for Angel and I. "I'm fine with my life Angel.

"Well, how will you write about the world if you haven't seen it?" Angel said.

"I can't see it anyway. So, what the hell!" I retorted, fighting back additional tears. Angel got up to leave, but before she left, she said,

"When are you going to see the world through your eyes?"

CHAPTER FIVE

"How They Began"

"There's a marked difference between acquaintances and friends. Most people really don't become friends. They become deep and serious acquaintances. But in a friendship, you get to know the spirit of another person; and your values coincide."

Maya Angelou

"I don't like it here already"

"Angel, give it a try. We just moved-in a month ago."

"When was the last time you've seen her move from the porch without an escort. I bet we have nothing in common. What kind of friendship is that? I'm not two. I don't want to hang out with her with her weird mother hovering.

"Well, that's a switch. So now you're open to hanging out?" Angel took a deep gulp of agitated breath.

"Yea, I guess."

"That's great, baby. You might be pleasantly surprised," said Mrs. Womack.

I felt like a big loser as I listened to Angel and her mother talk about me as if I wasn't standing two feet away. They really needed to learn how to whisper. I didn't want to be friends with her anyway. They all treated the blind and visually impaired like they were victims of some harsh consequence. I didn't need somebody around me feeling sorry for me, and treating me like I was handicapped. I could feel her sympathetic eyes looking at me. I wanted her and her mother to go back next door to their own house and leave me alone. I leaned into my mother's ear and actually whispered unlike my neighbors, and pleaded.

"Please tell them I'm not feeling well, Momma"

"Moon, give her a chance. Something is telling me she won't be like the others." Momma said with a consoling embrace. My mom gave me a subtle shove towards the smell of apple scented body mist and Chanel perfume. I stumbled a little, regained my balance, held my head up with confidence, and then walked towards the scents until they were accompanied with body heat and breathing.

"Hi! I'm Hope but my family and close friends call me Moon." The Chanel perfume spoke first.

"Hello Hope. It is very nice to meet you. You are so beautiful."

"Thank you. Nice meeting you too." The Chanel perfume faded into my mother's direction, but the apple body mist stayed.

"Hi," she said.

"Hi," I said.

"I'm Angel. What do people do for fun around here? We just moved here from Greenbelt, Maryland. Heard a lot about the city. Beltway Plaza Mall and rec centers are all we have for fun. I only come to DC to watch the Redskins play at RFK or the Bullets play downtown. My Daddy is a big sports fan."

"That sounds like fun. I'm not really into anything outside of home except school. I go to The Maryland School for the Blind. I do music club and History club. Stuff like that. Oh and no big deal, but I'm a mathlete.

"You're good at Math too? I got straight A's, and I'm taking Geometry in the seventh grade. So you got some competition, Boo. Music Club, huh? What's that like?" Angel's voice changed to reveal her enthusiasm. I smiled. My porch was really long with a bench on one side and two wicker chairs on the other. My mom and Mrs. Womack were sitting in them and belted out an occasional, "You don't say!" and "Oh My! Girl, stop!" While Angel and I sat and got more acquainted on the other side of the porch.

"Music club is like a band. I started it. I used to call it the Wonder Club after my favorite musician, Stevie Wonder but everyone thought I was buggin. Stevie Wonder is a decorated music Icon who happens to be blind, and they still didn't like the name. I was so annoyed. We use Braille to read music. There is a guitar player, violinist, drummer, and piano player. We also have a couple of MCs who think they're Doug E. Fresh, Salt N Pepa, and Run DMC all wrapped up into one."

"Sounds cool! What do you do there?"

"I write poetry which as you probably know music kinda is. We've turned a couple of my poems into songs, but I also play the keyboard a little."

"Homegirl, you are amazing! Am I allowed to come and hear you guys rehearse sometimes?" Angel asked excitedly.

"Yes, you can. Us blindies love to have sighted people around so we can show them how well we can see. It will be nice to hang out with you too." We laughed and kept talking as if no one else was around. I invited her to come in and the next thing I knew, I had a sighted friend.

"When you said History Club, I was thinking, she is a bigger nerd than me, but I get it now." Angel scanned my room looking at the many Helen Keller posters on my wall. "I get it, she was blind but so was Louis Braille. I don't see his poster," Angel inquired.

"Helen Keller was blind, deaf, and a woman. Every time I read her books; I stop feeling ashamed of my impairment.

"You read them more than once?"

"Of course. Every time I read her books; I feel unstoppable. She didn't let her impairments stop her from fighting"

"Fighting," Angel inquired.

"Fighting for equal rights for people like me, and all people. We don't want people feeling sorry for us and treating us like we're weak. We are strong. Someday I'm going to stand up for impaired people all over the world like she did," I declared.

"Yes, you are, Hope. I believe it," Angel said while putting her hand up signaling me to slap five. Her hand looked more like a shadowy figment but I could make out her fingers that were slightly spread out so I slapped five right back. Ms. Carol interrupted us letting Angel know she was going back across the grass path home and that she could stay a couple more hours if she wanted. "I really like the mall. Where is the closest one?" Angel inquired.

"I've been a couple of times with my family. I never really had fun. My mom always finds a seat somewhere for me while she shops for me. She always tells me that what she finds is stylish. I only believe her when I get a compliment. I've never window shopped or tried on clothes for fun like people our age do. Whenever I go into a store. My mom picks out what she thinks I'll wear and helps me try them on even though I don't want her to. I can do it myself. Maybe that's her way of making the situation less awkward. It's not fun at all. When I'm there, I can see some bright colors if the light is bright enough for me to use the contrasts. I can also feel the different kinds of fabric. I love perfume and candle shops too. And guess what?

"What?"

"I secretly want my own pair of high heel shoes."

"How high are we talking? I'm twelve. Ms. Carol will never go for it. She says, 'you have plenty of time for all of that when you're older," Angel stated mocking her mother. I started laughing so hard.

"Ms. Pranita says the same thing," I replied, barely getting the words out. Eventually, my laugh became contagious and Angel started giggling too. We couldn't stop.

After that day, Angel and I became inseparable. If she wasn't at my house, I was at hers. I became part of the family.

CHAPTER SIX

"The Mall"

"A lot of people resist transition and therefore never allow themselves to enjoy who they are. Embrace the change, no matter what it is; once you do, you can learn about the new world you're in and take advantage of it."

Nikki Giovanni

"Your mother said yes! I'm CISED!!! C'mon girl let's go to The *GAP* first. There is a jean jacket that looks so cute on me." Angel always talked about the latest fashions. At the moment it was bell bottom jeans or tight leg jeans and the coolest sneakers. Fila, New Balance, Tretorn, Converse, or Air Jordans by Nike. I never really knew what any of the outfits actually looked like on me, but Angel always looked me up and down and gave me her appraisal. I was a really cool artifact. Once I was told how stylish or cute I was, I was good as long as it came from Angel. Momma always bought me the latest gear. She really wanted me to fit in, but I never really did.

"I'm walking as fast as I can. I see very clearly, remember! You make it extra hard to walk with this big bag between us. What's it for?"

"As soon as we are out of your mother's sight, I'll let you know."

"Huh?"

"A few more steps. Now, stop right here. Give me this cripple stick"

"Wait! What are you doing?" Before Angel could answer, two of her friends from her old neighborhood showed up. The closest mall to my house was in a town called Hyattsville. The mall we shopped at was *Prince Georges Plaza*. Greenbelt, where Angel was from, wasn't that far away, so I wasn't surprised when she ran into somebody she knew.

"Hey Angel, are you hard up for friends? What are you doing with her? I mean she's pretty but uhh…"

"I'm so glad I can't see your ugly face, but I smell your stinky breath. Leave us alone, and go brush your teeth," I retorted with rage in my voice and fire coming out of my ears. I could hear the many bursts of laughter. As people walked by. I released my hands from my hips, and the smoke cleared from my ears and flared nostrils. Angel stood up after bending over in non-stop laughter.

"Malcolm, go away," Angel demanded.

"Yea, Malcolm go away," I parroted with agitation.

"This is a free country. I'll go wherever I want."

"Yea, well you are not wanted here so go away," declared Angel. I cooled off but kept my stance just in case I had to give him some more of my sass. I watched the annoying figures walk away and turned to face Angel. We had to move to the side because a mother and her little boys wanted to get a drink from the water fountain that we were standing in front of.

"Angel, why did we stop?"

"It's my 13th birthday. We're thirteen now. I want to have fun and maybe even talk to a few boys. Nobody is going to flirt with us with this stick in the way. Trust me. I got you. I will always have your back. You don't need this stick. I'm going to fold it up and place it in this bag."

"So how do I walk around? I don't come to this mall that much mainly because of people like him. So now you want me to walk without my stick, so I can trip and bump into stuff, and embarrass myself even more?"

"No! No! No! Trust me. I got you. I'm going to walk in front of you with my arm extended to the back. We're going to stroll in the direction of each store, and let you know if we're turning left or right. Follow my lead."

"Okay, but remember I took my glasses off so I could look cute, so I have to be crazy careful. I really only see shadows and grayish figments if it's not enough light. This is nuts, Angel!"

"I got you," Angel replied with reassurance. We started to walk and like a person just learning a complicated dance, I stumbled and tripped a few times. We had to stop once or twice, but finally I started to stay in rhythm. The GAP, our first store, had a little bit of a new clothing smell. I was really looking forward to feeling the fabrics. Anything bright colored and fuzzy or furry put a smile on my face."

"I found it, Hope. Yes, girrrl! I found the dark blue jean jacket of my dreams that looks so good on me," Angel shouted. After that shout came even more screams of happiness. Angel kept finding things that she loved. I was so excited for her but a part of me was jealous and wished I could help her look for outfits, try them on, see them and love them too. The shots rang out as Angel led me from store to store. Hecht's, Woodward and Lothrop, Lord and Tayler etc. Finally, I asked to sit. I needed to rest. I was also overcome with hunger. Angel sat down beside me and laid a white shopping bag on my lap. I looked at her blurred shaded face and smiled. I embraced the bag and gave Angel a hug.

"For me?

You're my girrrl!" She uttered. I was about to open the bag but Angel stopped me. She placed my hand on my pouch. That was her signal to go into my pouch to get my goggles, so I could see what she bought me a little clearer. I grabbed my glasses from my pouch and put them on. The bag made that crumbly noise bags make when you're opening them. I looked in and shouted with excitement and happiness. Every cool teen in the D.C. area had a pair of Guess jeans. I made out that familiar upside-down triangle we all lived for. After the jeans was the prettiest brightest yellow Guess sweatshirt.

"Thank you so much, Angel! How, I know our parents do okay, but where are you getting all of this money?"

"Most of what I bought today was on the sale rack, and my mom gave me a little extra to get you something," Angel revealed.

"I can't wait to try everything on. Do you think they will allow me to try this outfit on in Hecht's even if you have already purchased the clothes?"

"Cmon. You never know until you ask. This is the one time that being legally blind comes in handy. Follow my lead." Angel took my symbol stick out of her very large tote bag, and handed it to me. We walked over to the counter together and asked as polite and puppy dogish as we could.

"Excuse me ma'am?" Angel asked with a polite whisper.

"What can I do for you, sweetie," the associate replied. I interrupted. "Ummmm, would it be okay if I tried these on in the dressing room even though my sister already purchased them?" The associate took a pause, looked at us and then pointed towards the dressing rooms.

"The dressing rooms are in the far-right corner. You can't miss them. It's where all of the clothes are scattered here and there." I like when people talk to me like I'm sighted. Me and Angel headed to the dressing rooms. The associate was correct. I could faintly see patches of bright pinks, greens, and yellows all over the place. On the floor, across the doors and on the dressing room benches. Angel picked up a pile of a mixture of clothes, hangers and tags and placed them on the floor outside of my dressing room. I closed the door before she could reenter.

"What are you doing?" Angel inquired with a high-pitched expressive tone in her voice as if she was shocked.

"I dress myself, homegirl. What? You thought my mother still dresses me at thirteen?" I stated with confidence.

"Oh! So cool. Okay, I'm waiting out here for the big Vogue moment. Oh, and give me back that cripple stick."

"It's called a symbol stick or cane," I replied annoyed.

"Whatever! You're no cripple so I don't want you looking like one. Hand it over," Angel demanded. I lifted up the stick over the dressing room stall wall. Angel grabbed it and placed it in that big obnoxious bag of hers. For some reason I got nervous when it was time to get dressed. Taking off my clothes was never a problem, but putting them on was the challenge. Finding my hands and feet weren't always easy. I guess I just wasn't coordinated enough, so I made up a song to help me get dressed. I started reciting it in my head.

My outfit was on. I felt so cute and stylish. This outfit was fly and I knew it. I held my hands out to feel for the mirror. I found it. I needed my glasses so I could see the blurry but satisfying image of myself staring back at me. Luckily my pouch was right at the edge of the bench inside the dressing room stall. I put on my goggles, and just as I predicted, I was fly. Guess up and down, baby. Yeah!

"You finished?" Angel inquired

"Coming out now." I walked out with my goggles on so I could enjoy Angel's reaction. I started doing my, "I look good" dance. Angel laughed. "Don't I look fly?"

"Yes, girrrl. You look so fly. That yellow is poppin on you. I love it," Angel shouted with excitement.

"Yes, so fly. I agree."

"Okay, take it off so I can put it in the bag including those goggles. We need to go back to being cute at the mall so those goggles gotta go," Angel demanded. I got that Angel wanted us to be the cute duo at the mall, but the goggles statements were starting to hurt my feelings a little. I really didn't like other people referring to my glasses as goggles. Only me. I couldn't help it if I needed such a strong prescription. After that statement my confidence started diminishing. I wanted to cry while taking off the outfit, but I sucked it up and pretended to be okay. It was nice to be accepted for once. I didn't want to lose her friendship.

"Hey, all done. Put these back in the bag, please. I'm ready." I faked a smile and followed Angel holding her hand from the back of her. I finally learned her walking rhythm so I could keep up. By the time we got to the doorway, both our mothers were walking in our direction. I knew my mom's voice anywhere.

CHAPTER SEVEN

"Stone Community Pool"

"I really don't think life is about the I-could-have-beens. Life is only about the I-tried-to-do. I don't mind the failure but I can't imagine that I'd forgive myself if I didn't try."

Nikki Giovanni

No one sees underwater unless they want to. When my mom first introduced me to swimming, I was only seven. I was scared to death. The water just looked like it never ended. I read books about the Black Hole in space. The whole idea creeped me out. That's what the water looked like to me. I didn't see the blue pretty water that sighted people saw. My view was mostly grayish blue like looking at the pacific ocean on a foggy day. The water looked like a black hole covered in fog. My mom hired me a swim teacher who met us twice a week at The Stone Community indoor pool. I tried to see what my mom described - the beautiful botanical blue clear water divided in feet. She even jumped in to show me how harmless it was.

She said, "See baby nothing is eating me. There are no monsters here. Come in. You're going to love it." It was the large mouth of an animal ready to swallow me whole. I didn't want to even put a toe in its mouth. She ended up being right. Once I got in, I never wanted to get out. So, six years and four first-place medals later, there I was.

Swimming just came naturally to me. It felt like we were all on the same level: sighted, visually impaired, blind, deaf, etc. In the water, no one was a cripple.

I woke up one Saturday morning and called Angel.

"Hello," Angel answered.

"Hey, homie. What are you doing?"

"Eating Fruit Loops. Why?"

"Are you doing anything today?"

"I have to help clean the house, but after that, I'm free. Why?"

"Can you swim?" I inquired hoping for a yes. I closed my eyes while my stomach turned to knots. Swimming was one of my favorite things to do. Writing was my number one.

"A little. I just hate when the water burns my eyes so I wear swim goggles." She uttered the last part as if she was embarrassed.

"Let's go to Stone Pool today. It'll be fun." Angel paused and sighed.

"I guess so. I don't even know where my bathing suits are." Angel panicked. Everything we did, we had to be cute doing it.

"Okay cool. My mom said she'll take us at 2PM. Is that okay?" I asked.

"Yep. I'll be ready, Angel paused and stuttered a little while responding. It sounded like she was nervous.

The pool was surprisingly crowded. I spied fluorescent bikini bathing suits, boys wearing swim trunks or speedos. There were brown and beige bodies everywhere laying on reclining lawn chairs. There were even four lifeguards on duty. I wasn't used to going on the weekend. I met my coach on Mondays and Wednesdays for drills. Angel followed me in. Whenever she walked slowly that meant she was afraid or hesitant. Angel and I wore matching bikinis except hers was fluorescent blue and mine was green.

"What's wrong?" I asked with concern.

"Nothing. Well, I just haven't swum in a long time."

"Follow my lead. We got this. I grabbed Angel's hand and pulled her behind me toward my favorite spot near the 7 foot mark. She held onto the tips of my fingers until we arrived at the chairs.

"Are you okay hanging out here?"

"Sure," she shrugged in agreement. Angel placed her towel on one of the chairs and reached in her bag for her swim goggles.

"No, No, No, we have to be cute when we swim homegirl, so hand over those ugly goggles," I stated with a hint of payback in my voice. Angel laughed while placing her goggles back into her bag. I walked to the edge. I hit that ledge so much during my early years of training. I knew how to get to the edge before diving or jumping like a rockstar on that day. Splash! Splash! Splash! I jumped in. The water felt magical and warm. This was the most fun I had in the fog. "Jump in, Angel, do you want me to come out and get you?" I teasingly threatened.

"No, I'm coming in. Just getting used to the water."

"Okay, don't stay on the ledge for too long. I'm going to take a couple of laps. I wasn't used to so many limbs. People were everywhere. I could hear them and feel them as they moved through the water. They must've seen me because I didn't bump into anybody. I swam like a dolphin. I pushed through the water feeling it in my scalp and all over my body. My arms were tightly stretched out in front of me leading me like a tour guide. My body moved like a mermaid, feet flopping tightly together to give me more speed. Suddenly there were no limbs in the pool, it was as if it were only myself and the water. I kept my hands and arms stretched out to reach the pool wall. I had used my head too many times. I didn't want to feel that pain again. After two laps, I swam back to the 7 foot mark to find Angel talking to Marco, her crush. She was still sitting in the same spot. If looking cute was an Olympic sport she would win a gold medal

"Hi Marco."

"Hey, Hope."

"Angel, why are you still sitting in the same spot? Marco, help me pull her in." Angel tried to make a run for it but Marco caught her torso and I grabbed her legs." Angel screamed and laughed.

"STOP! I don't wanna swim. Stop ya'll. I don't wanna mess up my hair. Stop it you two. This blowout took me an hour."

"Why did you do a blowout to come to the pool?" I inquired, annoyed. Angel kept fighting and resisting. She just used her hair as an excuse not to try. She hadn't swam in a long time and

I wouldn't let her use her goggles, so I had to pull her. It was so hard to hold on to her legs while treading water but somehow, we got her in. She disappeared underwater for a few seconds. I got scared. She said she could swim and she sat at the 7 foot mark but I wasn't completely sure. She popped back up like a jack in the box and started splashing water at me and Marco. What a relief, I thought.

"Thanks! This water is warm. It feels good. You two play too much! I was gonna come in eventually." Angel dipped her head of curls into the water and jumped back in. I could see how the light from above gleamed against her fluorescent bikini.

"Let's see what you can do," I uttered while smacking my slanted head on the side to get the water out of my ears.

"Let's race. If you win. It's only because you won't let me wear my goggles, Angel uttered with competitive sassiness. She was kind of competitive. She hated to lose, especially to me. We found an empty space in the pool. Marco stood at the finish line to conduct the race.

"The first one to hit the wall and go back to the starting point wins bragging rights. Get on your mark. Get Set. Go," Marco yelled! I swam faster than when I competed in the state championships. I needed to prove myself. I was a fish. My feet and legs were moving in a swift up-and-down motion. My whole body moved with the water as if we were one. I kept telling myself to go, swim, move, faster, faster. I pushed bubbles out of my nose and hit the wall quickly, then back to the starting point. There was nothing on my mind but winning. I continued to move swiftly and quickly. One more big push and I was there.

When I emerged from the water the pool only contained me and Angel. Everyone else was watching the race. The next things I heard were shouts of yay! Way to go, Hope! You did it! You're a rockstar swimmer! That's the fastest swimming I've ever seen! I looked for Angel. She was three minutes behind me. She popped up out of the water and did the unexpected. She hugged me with excitement

"Yay! You did it. I'm so glad you won."

"Did you let me win because of my eyes, Angel?"

"No way. I gave it my everything. This is just your house, homegirl!!" Angel swam to the ledge and grabbed our towels.

"Thanks, just making sure," I replied with great satisfaction.

"Let's go. I'm hungry. My mom bought us a pizza from *Three Brothers. Angel announced. She and I started walking towards the locker rooms. When we were almost about to enter the doors, Marco and his friend Al yelled to get our attention.*

"Leaving so soon," Marco inquired to get our attention. I was so nervous because boys were not usually nice to me. I started walking again. Angel pulled my arm to get me to stop.

"Wait Hope. Let's talk to them"

"I thought you were hungry. Our moms are waiting in the car," I uttered.

"Cmon let's talk for two minutes," she stated with a begging whine in her voice.

"Hey Angel Face. Isn't that why your moms named you Angel?" said Marco.

"That and amongst other things." Angel was blushing while moving closer to Marco, her crush. My mother claimed my eyes might get stronger as I got older but they would never be 100%, so I couldn't really see how cute Marco was. Angel described him as dreamy. She said his green eyes and ginger complexion made him exotic. She said he was just tall enough, a little taller than her and she liked that he was on the track team at school. His friend Al's grayish dark shadow was moving in my direction. I started breathing really heavily and walked hurriedly into the locker room. Thank God I was familiar with the room so I leaned and hid behind the brick wall. I kept breathing trying to calm myself down. While hiding behind the wall I could hear the three of them talking.

"Why did she run from me?" Al retorted loudly.

"She's shy," Angel replied.

"She's really pretty," said Al.

"Call me later, Angel," said Marco.

"Maybe," Angel replied blushing. Angel walked into the locker room and found me barely calm and hiding behind the brick wall near the entrance of the locker room. She gave me a huge much needed hug. *"Are you okay, Hope? I'm so sorry Al scared you."*

"He didn't scare me, just the thought of talking to a boy I can't see scares me." I started crying and yelling. Angel tried to console me but I pushed her away. *"I can't see him,"* I shouted repeatedly. That's what scares me the most. How was I supposed to enjoy a conversation with a boy I can't even see?

"You do the thing you are talking about with me every day," Angel said assuringly.

"But that's different," I yelled. Angel embraced me while I cried out my frustrations.

"No, it is not different. It is not," Angel stated firmly.

CHAPTER EIGHT

"The dreaded Arcade"

"Mistakes are a fact of life.
It is the response to the error that counts."
Nikki Giovanni

It was my turn again to be unfamiliar. Angel's crush was going to be at the arcade. Most of the time boys followed her around like mice to peanut butter, but when it came to Marco, the cutest boy in our neighborhood, she melted like butter. I heard about Ms. Pacman but I'd never actually played it. So, I was a little curious when Angel begged me to ask my mom if she could take us.

The arcade was outside of the mall in a round glass building. Angel allowed me to wear my goggles in the car. Kids on skateboards slid down the metal banisters and all shades of skin and sneakers entered and exited with excitement. Playing those games was like a new addictive drug for kids our age. My mom was always nearby whenever Angel and I hung out. She finally found a parking space and walked us in.

"Yuk! Girl, it smells like thousands of stinky armpits. I'm leaving," I declared. Angel pulled me back beside her.

"Chill out! You'll get used to it. C'mon, I gotta find my Marco. I followed Angel holding on to her hand a little tighter than usual. My symbol stick was in her bag, and my goggles were sentenced to my pouch. It was so dark, but in every crevice and corner there were flashes of colorful light and sounds of dying video game men, and loud screams of players beating the latest high score. Because it was so dark, It was hard for me to follow and adjust to the rhythm of Angel's walk. I was completely impaired. I kept tripping over the back of Angel's brand-new Fila sneakers.

"Hope, stop stepping on my heels. What is wrong with you today?"

"HELLO! You're walking a legally blind girl around in the dark! This is so stupid let's go!" I retorted. Suddenly, Angel pulled me in the direction of what looked like a gigantic black ball. It turned out to be a large group of kids surrounding this one kid playing a game that had a bright yellow ball with a red bow on the screen. I heard sounds like,

"He just reached the next level!"

"He made it to 'The Chase'"

"Look at that high score!" Somehow Angel pulled me into the blob. The glass screen illuminated with a beautiful bright light that I could somewhat make out without my goggles. This little yellow thing with a red bow was quickly eating a bunch of pellets in rows placed all over the screen. The object was to get all the pellets without being eaten by these colored ghosts, You got three chances to get to different levels. Although, I think when you got to a certain number of points you could earn more of those little yellow ladies. I really wanted to play. I was mesmerized by the colors and the thrill of competing not with a person, but with the very large computer.

The player kept playing. He kept earning the little yellow ladies and the score grew more and more. For a brief moment I glanced at the player's face and I thought it was Marco. Someone cheered him on by calling him by name. It was Marco. I couldn't believe it. Everyone kept cheering loudly with every bitten pellet and every level reached, especially Angel.

"Look at my Marco, Hope, ain't he amazing. Do you see that Bumpin score?" Angel slapped me five.

While she was fixated on her man playing Ms. Pacman, I reached in her bag, pulled out my symbol stick, took my goggles out of my pouch, put them on and decided to check out the other games. I made it over to a green game that wasn't as bright, but It looked like it was called something with a Gal. The player was using a small stick to make a weapon that destroyed these little balls that spat back harmful fire. I made it to another game where there was a little orange fruit with a nose jumping on boxes. I was able to read that. It was called Qbert. I really wanted to play, but I didn't want the cool kids to make fun of me for doing it wrong or for not being able to read something right. So instead of trying, I fought through the darkness and ended where I thought Marco and Angel were. Instead, I ended up at a game that was really large. It looked like a huge box with a steering wheel. I leaned in over the box trying to see what was on the screen. I leaned too far over and my goggles fell off. Shoot! I shouted. They hit the person in the box.

"Don't worry. They didn't break," a familiar voice responded.

"Hi. Thank you" I looked up and came face to face with Al, Marco's friend from the pool. I quickly placed my glasses back in my pouch and leaned my symbol stick against the back of the big box.

"You look pretty. Hope, right?"

"Yes, Hope."

"Do you want to learn how to play this?"

"Yes, I mean no, I mean yes."

"Come on this side. I'll help you. You just have to sit in the seat and stretch out your legs. Place your left foot on the go pedal and your right foot on the stop pedal. When the car starts to move, you just have to keep it on the track and try not to crash before your time runs out."

"Thank you for explaining that. It sounds easy enough"

"May I sit next to you? I just want to be close by if you mess up and need my help. The box was wide enough for both of us to fit. When he sat next to me, it wasn't panic attack part two. I was surprisingly calm. It didn't matter that I couldn't see him. His voice was familiar and sweet. Al was kind enough to place a quarter into the game and as soon as we were snug next to each other and my foot touched the go pedal, I heard another familiar voice.

"Hope! Hope! Where are you?

"Over here, Momma"

"Thank God! I was keeping track of you for a while there and then I lost you. Everything okay? Who is this young man?"

"Mom, this is Al. He was helping me with this game."

"I see. Nice to meet you, Al. Where is Angel, Hope?"

"The last time I checked she was over at the Ms. Pacman game." My mother stuttered and paused. She seemed confused.

"It's the one with the yellow ball and red bow."

"Oh okay, I see her. Angel, come on, sweetie, momma summoned Angel and I to go.

"Hope, make sure you have all of your stuff." Thank God she didn't say glasses and symbol stick. I would've died in front of Al.

"Did you girls have fun? Whooooh, it really stinks in that place. I don't see how you two could stand it" Angel and I laughed.

"You get used to it," Angel replied.

"I will never get used to that, Angel"

"I get it, Ms. Pranita." Angel laughed. She and I sat in the back so we could talk about the day's events. I was really happy when my mom put on the radio. I was hoping she couldn't hear us over WHUR.

"So, what happened with you and Marco?" I inquired.

"Girl, nothing. He was way more interested in his silly high score than he was with me. I cheered him on anyway. That's what girlfriends do," Angel stated bragging.

"Girlfriend? Are you guys going together? When did this happen? Wait. Does this mean you are steady with Marco? You can't talk to any other boys?"

"Yes. That's exactly what it means. My first boyfriend," Angel declared.

"Wow, I'm so excited for you, Angel. How did he ask? Wait, when did he ask?"

"Well, I called him after the pool and we have been talking daily since then. He asked yesterday and I told him I would give him my answer at the arcade."

"Now I see why you dragged me to that stinky place." Angel laughed and continued.

"While he was reaching his big-time high score. I leaned over and whispered in his ear, yes. After that, he was unstoppable. He didn't stop winning until Ms. Pranita called me to go. True story."

"I don't believe it," Angel laughed and tapped my arm.

"It's true. Now what about you and that stick of yours. Somehow it escaped from my bag."

"It was dark in there, homie. I needed my stick and my goggles."

"Oh no! Not those goggles, Hope.

"Yes, I wore my glasses. I am legally blind. Guess who sat beside me while I played the car race game?"

"Goodie, Al sat next to you? Wait, you played one of the games? Yes, and I would've won both the game and him if my mother hadn't found me." Angel laughed and agreed.

"Hope, tell me more. I want all the details, girlfriend.

"Well, I made my way to three different games with the help of my friends, glasses and symbol stick. When I got to the race game, I leaned over the box where you sit to play, and my glasses fell off. Al just happened to be seated in the box when they fell off, and he caught them or picked them up off of the floor. One of the two, I'm not sure. Then he offered to teach me how to play the game."

"He really likes you, Hope. He said you are really pretty when we were at the pool."

"Yes, I overheard you guys talking when I panicked and ran."

"Time to go home and get ready for the school week, Moon. Angel, tell Carol I said hello," my mom stated rudely, cutting off the best part of the conversation. I wanted to hear more about Al thinking I'm pretty.

"Okay, I will. Thanks for taking us to the arcade. Do you think Hope and I can be dropped off alone next time?"

"Not on your life," my mom exclaimed with a little bit of a subtle annoyance to her voice.

"Okay, Ms. Pranita. I understand." Angel walked up her porch stairs. My mom waited for her to get in and then parked in our driveway. I always enjoy being with Angel but I was definitely ready to go home to my journal and posters. I made my way to my room, pulled off my socks and shoes, and laid vertically across my full-size bed. A little bit later my mother showed up and laid beside me. She was lying vertically as well.

"Moon," she said in that endearing yet stern tone.

"Yes, Momma." Why weren't you wearing your glasses or using your symbol stick today?" I shifted from being propped up on my chin to laying on my pillow on the side of my face.

"Angel and I decided that our duo is cuter without them. She said she would always protect me. We just want to look cute. Boys like me without them, momma"

"Moon, your glasses and your stick are used to keep you safe. I love you, and I know that you know how amazing you are just the way you are. Anybody who can't accept you the way that you are, is not the kind of friend you want to have. Angel is putting your life at risk. I want you to think about the importance of liking yourself first before you change so somebody else will like you."

"Momma, Angel is fine with my glasses and stick. She just doesn't like for me to wear them in public."

"Moon, do you like yourself?"

"Yes."

"Then you need to talk to Angel about just how much." My mom gave me a kiss goodnight and left me thinking about who is more important.

CHAPTER NINE

"The Rally"

"In the End, we will remember not the words of our enemies, but the silence of our friends..."

Martin Luther King Jr.

Bailey was coming out of the bathroom, so I asked him to walk Angel to the door for me.

"Bye, Angel," I said. "Call me tomorrow." Angel had me thinking in a way that I shouldn't have been. I wanted to go to the rally. I wanted to do something my parents would disapprove of. I needed to do this. I had to prove to myself that I could be independent. This acquittal is an unfair decision, and I must protest. My voice should be heard, I thought.

It made me think about when Momma and I visited Aunt Addie. She lived in Cape Charles, VA, a town down south in North Hampton County.

Once Daddy, Benny, and Bailey packed the back seat of Momma's 92 Honda Civic with a couple of suitcases, and a cooler full of fried chicken, potato salad, fruit salad, Cheetos, and juice boxes, Momma and I stopped at a Texaco to get gas. Then we hit Route 50 towards the Bay Bridge. I was excited. I started to put on my Walkman, but Momma instantly became beautifully reminiscent as usual.

"Moon?"

"Yes, Momma." I looked her way. She was seated upright, eyes on the road, and holding the steering wheel. Her eyes left the road for a brief second to look at me with that sweet smile she would always give me when she was happy or comfortable. Her eyes turned back to the road. She grabbed her water without taking her eyes off the road and took a long gulp.

"Ahhhh, that's refreshing," she said, smacking her lips.

"Never take the rights you have today for granted." I looked at her solemnly while slightly distracted by all the noises outside of the car on the road. Because when one sense weakens, you start to rely on your other senses more, so the brain does a magic trick in your head that makes the other senses crazy reliable. My hearing and sense of smell became super powerful. I started getting distracted by every rock and gravel Momma drove over. I listened to the tractor trailers a few cars behind us, making their way up to pass us. I listened to every gugonk, gugonk, gugonk that the vehicles made rolling over a random pothole on the road.

"I won't, Momma," I answered.

"Moon, I want you to understand that not all White Americans are like the ones who make the choice to discriminate against us. There were plenty of White Americans who fought for African Americans to have civil rights. People from all walks of life, all races, and socioeconomic backgrounds helped to fight injustice. Yes, they were majority Black, but there were also White, Brown, rich, poor, it didn't matter. Anybody with human decency joined the fight. Those who cared about human rights marched and fought so that you could have equal rights today. As I said, we were the majority, but others cared."

"Yes, Momma. You're right. That's why I like Helen Keller. She didn't just fight for the blind or deaf" I said confidently.

"Yes. Some whites marched to Selma. Whites attended the March on Washington. There were even White Freedom Riders." I gasped.

" I didn't know that, Momma."

"Yes indeed," She affirmed.

In 1964 James Chaney, a Black man, Andrew Goodman, a White man, and Michael Schwerner, another White man, went down to Longdale, Mississippi, to try to help folks down there register to vote. Black people had been disenfranchised for over 70 years. You know, left out of stuff. There were a couple of organizations dedicated to helping us vote. Those three men were members of the Council of Federated Organization (COFO). Your aunt Addie was a member of the Student Non-violent Coordinating Committee. They worked on this cause too, but not in Mississippi. Addie can tell you all about it once we get down there.

"Disenfranchised?" I asked.

"That means being denied their rights so that they will feel disconnected or set apart from the majority."

"Oh. Okay." I knew that, but sometimes I like to make Momma feel smart. I dislike being a know-it-all just because I skipped two grades. Nobody likes a smartass.

These nice fellows went down there to meet with a church congregation after the Klan had burned it down. They were also working with the Freedom Summer Campaign that was set up to try to register Black voters. Back then, as you may know, the local governments set up legal blocks on voting that they knew Blacks could not bypass. Momma appreciated her Oldies stations on the radio. I loved this music, too, even though it was way before my time. The radio was set to Memories 104.5 FM. Sam Cooke's "A Change is Gonna Come" started playing.

"Ooooooo! That's my song," Momma said, nodding her head and humming the tune. Sam Cooke sang! Momma shouted with a joyful moan and hum.

"I was born by the river in a little tent

Oh, and just like the river I've been running ever since

It's been a long time, a long time coming

But I know a change gonna come, oh yes it will...."

I agreed with him. A change was gonna come, but we couldn't just assume it would happen on its own. We had to do something about it. And I didn't mean the Black Panther movement, I didn't want to be that radical, but I wanted to be heard. Be a contributor to the change, I thought.

Yea. Those poor fellows spent quite a lot of time down there in Neshoba County. Momma continued. *Enough time to* cause a threat. *Like the four officers acquitted today, the police officers in Longdale unlawfully hurt and, in this case, murdered helpless people and got away with it.* Sam Cooke continued,

"It's been too hard living, but I'm afraid to die Cause I don't know what's up there, beyond the sky...."

Momma went on as the air outside got thinner. We were crossing the Bay Bridge; so much water! It looked calm but scary. I saw figures of boats on the water. There was something about sailing that was mysterious to me. I guess it was hoping for something better on the other end when the boat stopped.

Momma continued, "It was such a shame. As Chaney, Goodman, and Schwerner were leaving, the three of them were pulled over in Philadelphia, Mississippi, for speeding. Momma took her hands off the wheel for a brief second and made air quotes using both sets of her pointer and middle fingers. I chuckled.

"They arrested them and held them in a holding cell for several hours. After their release, they kept on trying to leave Neshoba County. While they were driving, they were followed by police officers and the Ku Klux Klan. Some of the police officers were Klan members themselves. Well, the poor young men were pulled over again, but this time they abducted them. Those hateful spirits shot them and buried their bodies. It was a high-profile case, too. The FBI and the United States Navy were part of the search party. I hate to admit this, but it wouldn't have been that important if all of the victims were Black." I sat speechless. Helpless.

"Did they find their bodies, Momma?"

"Yes. But only after two months of unknowing. I can only imagine what their families went through. Racism and hatred are cancers that have spread all over this country, but it was so much worse in the South.

Like many cases involving White officers and Black victims, the officer got off. It was discovered that the Neshoba County Sheriff's Office and the Philadelphia, Mississippi Police Department were among the suspects. The State of Mississippi refused to prosecute. The Federal Court finally convicted some of them for civil rights violations, but I'm sure the punishment was minimal. A disgrace!" She retorted.

The lyrics of Sam Cooke's song kept lingering in my head. *"Change is gonna come, oh yes, it will."* He sounded so confident singing that last line—something I needed to have, confidence. I needed to believe that my strength was rooted beyond my eyes, but I just couldn't. Sitting and doing nothing while reflecting on injustice was one thing, but moving and making a difference was another. My apprehension and my militance had a fight inside my head. One of them won.

I abruptly pressed the button on my Walkman to stop the music, and before I could stop myself, I was walking carefully along the grassy man-made path we created from years of going to and from each other's homes. I did it. I rang Angel's doorbell.

CHAPTER TEN

"On My Own, The Rally Part Two"

"The only thing worse than being blind is having sight but no vision..."

Helen Keller

"Wait, Hope!" Angel yelled.

"I'm afraid you may trip and fall. It's starting to get a little dark out here. HOPE!"

"Yes," I answered, agitated and sliding my symbol stick across the sidewalk, making puffs of dust and disturbing empty cans.

"Wait, I know you are excited, but you want to get there alive. Don't you? Soon you won't be able to see in front of you at all. Do you even know where the Student Center is?" Angel asked. She was always trying to protect me. She was my unofficial bodyguard. When someone cut me off while I was walking or said anything rude to me, she became the epitome of an angry Black woman, except she was technically not a woman yet. I was just as sassy, but Angel was always jumping in to save the day before I could even part my lips to read'um their rights.

"No," I answered. "But with the adrenaline stored in me right now, I'm sure I'll find it."

"Girl, you are a trip!" Angel replied, laughing. When Angel and I stepped off the escalator at the Van Ness DCU Metro train stop, I could hear echoed, microphoned voices leading chants like "NO JUSTICE, NO PEACE" and "THE PEOPLE UNITED WILL NEVER BE DEFEATED".

There were people everywhere. Angel and I started walking towards the sea of students carrying picket signs. I could only see specks of the beige bricks of the Student Center. The students and the brick wall became one. It became a mosaic of color, words, movement, and voices. I looked to either side of me, and all I could make out were bits of words and clenched fists attached to erect arms raised with strength and passion. They were a pack of wolves, and justice was their prey. I knew the black unity fist anywhere. Momma told me all about that. It symbolized the Black Panther movement of the sixties and seventies. My mother wasn't a Black Panther but fought for the power of justice, Black or Non-Black.

As I continued to examine my surroundings, the portrait included words painted on hundreds of signs. I moved slowly and cautiously through the crowd. In the center, I saw Brutality. To the right, "Stop," and to the left, "No Beating." Further left, "King." I finally felt comfortable. Not seeing clearly in front of me did not stifle my voice. Suddenly I started, "No Justice, No Peace," softly to myself. I repeated twice more after taking a deep breath. Louder, I chanted, NO JUSTICE, NO PEACE! Through my excitement, my symbol stick fell from my hand. Damn! I muffled under my voice, but I didn't let that stop me. I froze for a second. Nervousness took over my body like a familiar invader. I thought, if I could get to the front where it was lighter, I could find Angel. With both hands stretched out in front of me, I moved closer to the sounds ringing from the microphones and echoed voices. I kept moving closer toward the voices. I couldn't see anything. It became pitch black in my world. As I shuffled forward, I heard a voice whispering beside me, "What is she, the bride of Frankenstein?" Muffled laughter followed.

"Why is she walking with her hands like that?" I stopped chanting. I dropped my hands. I was angry and embarrassed. I started walking hurriedly; I was frightened and frantic. I felt my chest tighten as my eyes welled with tears. I kept moving. I continued bumping into protestors. My head got heavy all of a sudden.

"Hey, watch where you are going!" said someone. The crowd was obviously on edge. This was a protest against brutality.

I stopped and leaned forward with both hands resting on my knees. "Are you okay?" said someone else. My anxiety caused me to get very dizzy. I lost my balance and tripped over a bottle or something left in the street. I slammed into the person in front of me. I grabbed their shirt so I wouldn't fall on the ground.

"Hey do you need help?" said the person I used for balance.

"No, I'm okay, thanks," I uttered with a cracked voice while fighting to hold back tears.

"Ouch! My foot!" Someone shouted as I stepped heavily on them with my Timberland boots. I stopped. The space started to swallow me like a shark swallowing its prey. I started to breathe more heavily.

"No Justice, No Peace!", "Ouch!", "You, okay?", "My foot!" The words replayed repeatedly in my mind like a broken record. My chest was tighter. I became paralyzed. I placed my hands over my ears. I couldn't make it stop. I screamed. I started staggering through the crowd screaming, staggering, screaming, staggering. People moved voluntarily. I cried out.

"HELP!" I kept screaming and staggering. My ears started to ring. "What's wrong?" uttered concerned voices. I continued staggering until I tripped over the foot of a bystander. I felt light, motionless, and then, THUMP! Suddenly all went silent, and then I heard sounds again. A shout rang out. "Help her!"

"We need an ambulance!" I could hear faintly, but I could not speak or see. Suddenly my body calmed. Somebody was carrying me. I felt far from the ground. The arms felt broad. Strong.

"Place her here," someone said.

"Are you okay?" A concerned voice said to me. It was a male voice like the baritones my Momma imitated but better. It was so dark that I couldn't see any part of his face, but his breath smelled like Pepsi and spearmint gum. The moment was a second, but it felt like an hour. I don't know what came over me, but I grabbed hold of his face using my thumbs to explore the shape of his eyes, cheekbones, and soft but masculine skin. He didn't retaliate. He allowed me to intrude his space freely, so I continued my examination. I gently pulled his ear to my lips.

"I'm blind," I uttered softly.

"And beautiful," he said. I blushed.

"Thank you," I said. "Will you help me up?"

"Sure," he said.

"Don't move her," said a concerned and authoritative voice.

"Who is that?" I inquired.

"An EMT," he replied gently, holding me down so I wouldn't move.

"She could be injured. Leave her there," said the EMT. My knight in shining armor gently placed my head back on his jacket. It smelled of Lagerfeld cologne. Mmmmmm! I was so entranced with his scent that I forgot where I was and what was happening. Because of the bright lights from the emergency vehicles, I could see Angel and other police officers clearing the crowd around me.

"Hope? Hope, are you okay? Can you hear me?" said Angel. I could hear the panic in her voice. I coughed. I was breathing normally. My chest loosened.

"I'm fine," I said. Angel lifted my head a little off the ground to hug me.

"Please don't move her," the EMT repeated.

CHAPTER ELEVEN

"The Hospital"

"The ultimate measure of a man is not where he stands in moments of comfort and convenience, but where he stands at times of challenge and controversy …"

Dr. Martin Luther King Jr.

I was back in a hospital room surrounded by a team of doctors. Momma had that same apprehensive look on her face that she described so vividly during the story of my birth. Any head trauma could harm my vision. I was afraid to face my Momma and Daddy.

"How are you feeling, Baby?" said Momma. She rubbed the top of my hair gently as a tear rolled gently down her cheek.

"You scared us, Moon," said Daddy.

"I'm fine, Daddy. I'm sorry I scared you guys, But I can't just stand around and do nothing while cops are getting away with attempted murder."

"I don't think they tried to kill him, but I certainly understand how you drew that conclusion," said Momma. I looked at my mother with confusion. I sat up, wearing a white hospital gown. I could feel the cool air hit my exposed back. My Daddy sat in the chair next to the door and the mounted TV.

"Calm down, Baby. You just experienced trauma. Try to keep calm. Let's talk about it later," Momma said.

"No," I exclaimed. "Let's talk about it now. I can't pretend that four white cops didn't get away with brutally beating a helpless black man. The video was clear, so America did not uphold its promise of justice for all. The days of Emmit Till are gone. I will not be afraid to fight. Blind or not. I won't be a cripple, and I won't be a bystander."

"Hope, you could have been killed out there today," Momma retorted. "What good are you to anybody, dead? I agree that what happened to that young man is wrong, but you must consider your health and well-being."

"Dr. Martin Luther King said, *'The ultimate measure of a man is not where he stands in moments of comfort and convenience, but where he stands at times of challenge and controversy.'* Today I showed my measure, and it won't be the last time," I declared. The nurse walked in.

"Hi. Sorry to interrupt, but it's time to take Alexandra for her CT Scan."

"Oh, Okay. No problem," said Momma. I started to step off of the bed. The room started to move. I slipped slightly off balance, and my mother caught me. I moved her hand. "I'm fine, Momma," I said, frustratingly. The nurse extended her hand to help as well.

"A little dizziness is normal with head trauma," said Nurse James. "Are you okay to walk?"

"Yes," I said.

"Okay, hold my arm as we walk." She extended her elbow, so I could hold onto her arm tightly.

I walked with her down a long hallway crowded with adults in white lab coats and stethoscopes wrapped around their necks. I could see clearer than usual, I guess because of the bright fluorescent lights that lined the ceiling. I repeatedly experienced slight pauses as we walked down the long hallway giving an occasional nod or hello to the many white coats moving in my direction. We finally found a straight path with a left turn into a less-lit room with a big space-capsule-looking machine.

"Do I have to get in that?" I inquired.

"Yes, but I promise it won't hurt," Nurse James stated. She gave me a reassuring smile and then checked my body for piercings or other jewelry I might've been wearing. "No jewelry in the tube. Do you have any, Honey?"

"No," I said. I got my ears pierced when I was really young, maybe one or two years old. My Momma said earrings made me look like a living doll. I did have them on at the rally, but I didn't know what happened to them. I always wore big silver hoops. They made me look Afrocentric.

"Okay, honey, step up into the tube and lie very still." I was a roll of cookie dough. "You'll be in here for about 30 minutes. Feel free to take a nap or think of rainbows. Did you know a rainbow means God is with you? He never fails us, honey," said Nurse James. I was shocked to hear her speak of God until I thought about it. I was at Immaculate Hospital. It was a Catholic hospital, so it wasn't uncommon to have religious staff.

My Momma and Daddy prayed all the time. They taught my brothers and me to pray too. We attended Greater Apostle Paul Baptist Church most Sundays. I wished Momma would've taken us more regularly. At a young age, I discovered the power in staying connected to the Lord.

I thought about that power while lying in the tube, the protective blanket placed over me made me feel warm and cozy, like God's protection. I thought I would be freaking out, but I wasn't. I closed my eyes.

"Ouch, my foot!" "Are you okay?" My mind drifted back there outside of the Student Center. Scared and anxious from the darkness and part of the crowd of protestors. I was alone but surrounded by hundreds of corn-rolled heads, afros, brown, caramel, ginger, mocha, and white skin tones. I thought about many sets of hands holding signs and fists of Black solidarity, and My hands extended forward, feeling my way in front of me with a blind girl's stance. I was alone. No mother. No father. No brother. No Angel.

No Angel! I opened my eyes. Where did Angel go? I was puzzled. I realized feeling helpless was no fun at all. I also realized that no one was going to always be there for me, and that only I can be there for myself! It seemed like people and strangers would only help you if you were on the ground, just like Rodney King. It wasn't until I was on the ground, hurt and helpless, that anybody decided to help me. It wasn't until

Rodney hit the ground smothered with kicks and batons that we decided to help him.

The guy who helped me was strong. He also smelled real good! I wondered if he was my age.. We were all there to give King a voice after witnessing his brutal beating on news sources everywhere; his helpless body was lying there in a fetal position. People only come to your rescue when you are literally down and out, I thought. While lying in that tube, wondering and reflecting, I decided that from that day forward I was going to take care of myself, but with my parent's financial support, of course. They loved doing that part, and I loved allowing them.

"Time to go, honey," Nurse James said. She extended her hand, but I ignored it. I got out of the tube by myself. I remembered my surroundings. I turned right into the fluorescent light, and led Nurse James back to my room. I slowly and carefully walked over to my bed and sat myself down.

CHAPTER TWELVE

"Recovery"

Nurse James wanted to speak to my parents privately.

"Mr. and Mrs. Nielson, would you mind following me to the waiting area? It's just two doors down."

"Yes. Of course," replied Momma. "Stay here, Hope. We will be right back."

"Okay, Momma," I said. I lied. I let them get a safe distance. As usual, Daddy was moving slowly. I waited and then followed them from a safe distance down the hall to a private area in the emergency room area. I waited until they closed the curtain, and then I hurried and stood as close as I could to the curtain.

"Have you ever heard of a vision coach?" Asked Nurse James.

"No, we haven't," Momma replied. Daddy grunted in agreement.

"Well, a vision coach is like a nurse who will come to your home two or three times a week to help Alexandra become more independent. Think of Anne Sullivan for Helen Keller."

"I see. Continue, please," said Momma.

"Yes. This nurse or coach, whatever you want to call her, will come to your house and help Alexandra learn to make her surroundings work for her. She will teach her to prepare meals, do her laundry, catch public transportation, etcetera," said Nurse James.

"Is that so?" Daddy stated with intrigue.

"Yes. She will teach Alexandra just about anything that she is not currently doing independently," explained Nurse James.

"This sounds expensive," Daddy said. Nurse James looked at my file.

"I see in her file that your insurance will cover it, so it shouldn't cost you a dime."

"Did you hear that, Pearson?" Momma said.

"Yes, I did," said Daddy.

"Okay. How do we get started?" asked Momma.

"You don't have to do a thing. Now that I know it's a go, I will put the wheels in motion. I will be in touch. I think Alexandra is ready for her independence," declared Nurse James.

"I think so, too," said Momma.

I got back to my room as fast as I could. I felt like crawling. That was how desperate I was to beat my parents back to the hospital room. I could feel Momma and Daddy coming my way, but I hurried back, ignoring them. I laid in my hospital bed, and out of nowhere, this spirit of apathy came over me. I didn't care if they spotted me or not. They soon entered the room. "Take care, Alexandra. As long as your CT scan is normal, you will be released tomorrow, but I won't be here tomorrow, so nice meeting you," Nurse James said endearingly.

"Nice meeting you, too," I replied.

"So, I take it you heard what we were talking about?" Momma inquired.

"Yes, I did, and I like the idea," I said with a big grin.

"Good. Nosey Rosey," Momma teased as she touched my nose with her pointer finger. "Your Daddy and I are going to get ready and go now. We will be back in the morning. Get some rest, Moon," Momma said.

"Okay, Momma, I will." Daddy kissed my forehead, and then they left.

At that moment, my Helen Keller biography came to life in my head. You see, Helen wasn't able to access two of her senses. She was fully blind and deaf. This is why she was my hero. Despite those two very restrictive disabilities, she became a prominent activist for human rights.

The most important part of the story is that she started completely reliant on her family members like me, but God sent her help. Anne Sullivan was her teacher.

She taught her things that allowed her to help herself. Anne Sullivan taught Helen how to communicate her needs through sign language. Water was her first successful word. Who could ever forget that? She also taught her manners and discipline, which helped to shape her into a role model for people like me. She received Anne Sullivan. I wondered who I would receive? I wondered what she would teach me? I already had manners. I attended the Maryland School for the Blind. I learned how to read Braille there and socialize with other kids. I learned discipline there, too, as well as at home. Pranita, aka Momma, was crazy strict about us being obedient. I'm surprised she didn't have more to say about me listening in on her, Daddy, and Nurse James's conversation. I guess she took it easy on me since I was in the hospital.

I hoped my Anne would teach me how to catch public transportation and overcome my anxiety about walking alone in my neighborhood. I wanted to attend the next rally with confidence. I wanted to be free. I hoped my Anne would liberate me!

The next morning, I awakened with a new outlook on life. The nurse brought in my breakfast. It was something yellow and white that looked like scrambled eggs, a dry piece of toast with no jelly or butter, and unseasoned grits. I was too excited to eat, so I used a single piece of toast to make a half-egg sandwich and drank the apple juice. Momma came in after I shoved the last of my sandwich in my mouth.

"Good morning, Moon," she said.

"Good morning, Momma."

"Did the doctor come in to see you yet?"

"No, not yet. No news is good news. Right, Momma?"

"I suppose, Moon. I suppose."

Dr. Renowski was a tall, stocky man who didn't wear a lab coat. He came in with his clipboard; he was wearing only a shirt, a dark necktie, and pants. He entered the room with a huge smile on his face. That was always a good sign. Doctors had been looking inside my pupils for years. I knew a face bearing good news from one bearing bad news, and he was bearing good news.

"Good morning, Mr. and Mrs. Nielson."

"Good morning, doctor," Momma and I replied in unison.

"I am Dr. Renowski. I had the pleasure of meeting your daughter last night," he said."

Yes, I heard," replied Momma.

"Well, I have reviewed the images from the CT scan, and everything looks normal. I also examined her eyes last night, and nothing has changed," he reported. Momma was relieved to hear the news, and so was I. My eyes were no longer a burden. I knew I would never fully regain my eyesight. I was just glad it didn't get worse.

"Can I go home now?" Momma gestured yes with a head nod. She extended her hand to grab mine. I pulled back rejecting the gesture, placed my glasses on my face, assembled the symbol stick Angel recovered from the Student Center parking lot, and allowed it to guide me out of the hospital.

CHAPTER THIRTEEN

"The Coach"

"We delight in the beauty of the butterfly, but rarely admit the changes it has gone through to achieve that beauty."

Maya Angelou

I was expecting my new vision coach to show up wearing a white high-collared ruffle blouse, a pencil skirt, buckled shoes, and glasses. I expected her to be the spitting image of Anne Sullivan, but she was not. Ms. Maverick wore light to dark contrasting colors, so I could always easily identify her. The day she came, she wore a pink, silk button-down shirt and black slacks with a skinny, hot pink belt running through her belt loops. I spotted her right away. She was a thin, frail black woman with thick coils of black dreads. She spoke with a southern accent, maybe Georgia or South Carolina, and she spoke so eloquently. She was quite the picture of intelligence.

The first thing she did when she entered the large compacted living room was pull out her measuring tape. She didn't even say hello to me. I thought that was strange after she spoke to my parents on the front porch for ten minutes. I was the main attraction, and she didn't even acknowledge me. She measured the distance between my Daddy's recliner and the coffee table. She measured the distance from one end of the living room to the next.

"Hello, Alexandra."

"Hello. Everyone just calls me Hope. You may, too," I replied.

"Okay, Hope. Your living room is approximately 500 square feet. The distance between that recliner and the coffee table is 30 inches. I have a measuring tape so you are able to accurately count paces. Did you already know that? Are you familiar with the square footage of the rooms and areas of your home?"

"No. I'm not," I said. "As long as it's daylight, I'm fine. In the dark, I feel around from one piece of furniture to the next."

"Enough of that. You must know your surroundings. It should be second nature to you. Measurements, floor plan, etc."

"I know the floor plan," I interrupted.

"That's good." Ms. Maverick looked at me from head to toe. "I take it you were not in a hurry to go anywhere this morning."

"I was. I had a class at the University this morning," I said.

"Then why are you wearing laces? You are not crippled or handicapped. You have a vision deficiency, so you must make choices to ensure efficiency. Purchase more shoes that you can slip your feet into—especially on days that you have classes or appointments unless you enjoy getting up an hour early." I started thinking. How did she know I had to wake up an hour early? How did she know shoestrings could be a challenge at times? I was impressed.

She carried her measuring tape all around the house, reporting the square footage of each room to me. I wasn't planning on giving her a full tour of our house, but since she insisted, I gave her one during her measuring frenzy.

"Know your surroundings. Recall distances intuitively," she said as she used her measuring tape to gauge distances from wall to wall and room to room.

She examined me again from head to toe. "Perfect hairdo. Short and choppy. Very efficient. Low maintenance."

"Thank you. I agree. It is easy for me."

"It's not about easy. You are not a cripple. You don't have to shy away from challenging situations, but efficiency is the goal. How can you make mundane tasks less complicated, so you have more time to dedicate to living your life."

"I like that," I replied.

"Stop slouching. You are beautiful. Stand up straight with confidence," she demanded.

I had developed poor posture from leaning on furniture to feel my way around when needed. Also, when not being led by another human being, I become anxious and fearful of missing a step or injuring myself. It was fear. Fear held me back. I was seventeen, and I acted like a three-year-old. I started ignoring Ms. Maverick and living more in my head. She started sounding like the teacher on a Charlie Brown special. My Momma once told me my middle name was Hope because she hoped I would be healthy, strong, and courageous. She always believed that all things are possible through prayer, and so do I. However, I also believed all things happened for a reason. My aunt Addie called me an old soul. I was way too profound for a teenager.

Ms. Maverick explained that in the outside world, nobody will change things to accommodate you unless they were paid to do so. She explained that I had to adapt to my surroundings by becoming extremely familiar, establishing consistent routines, and sticking with them.

Each day she came back. Each day I learned something new. We became friends.

We started in the kitchen. She began with a sharp pronunciation, "Hope, this is your kitchen."

"This is my kitchen," I repeated. She led me from the left of the kitchen to the right. Just like when we read or write a sentence from left to right. She placed my hands on the refrigerator and the handles and said, "refrigerator." Light or dark, this is where the refrigerator is, and these are the handles." She continued, again from left to right. "Ice maker, freezer. Shelf one: milk, water, juice. Shelf two: eggs, cold cuts, cheese, bacon, and hotdogs. Shelf three has two drawers filled with vegetables and fruit," she recited. Her voice sounded rhythmic like a song.

Ms. Maverick explained the importance of tapping into my other senses. "In the kitchen, Hope, it is important to use your sense of touch, smell, and hearing. Be in tune with hearing food boiling or popping on the stove. Also, listen for running or dripping water from the sink. Smell the individual vegetables, fruit, and other food items to identify them correctly." She went on. "These are the cabinets."

"These are the cabinets," I repeated.

"Bottom shelf, short drinking glasses, second shelf, coffee mugs, third shelf, tall drinking glasses, and wine glasses," she said. I repeated her entire statement in my head. I whispered to myself, "bottom shelf short drinking glasses. . .."

Ms. Maverick went on to the sink area. She started again from left to right, "Sink," she said. "Left knob is hot water, and the right knob is cold water. Here is the spigot," she said. She continued moving on to the stove. She introduced the rear burner knobs, front burner knobs, broiler and bake knobs. After the long and meticulous introductions, she suggested we take a break.

"Find a seat and sit down," she said. Things were quite fuzzy. I wasn't wearing my glasses, at Ms. Maverick's suggestion, I might add. I started with the table. I always knew where the table was because it was closest to the doorway, along the yellow, push-button, wall-mounted phone. My Momma always bragged that the table was her Salvation Army find. She said it had a few marks on it, but it was just like new. She placed a floral tablecloth on it. The yellow daisies matched well with the phone. I walked towards the door slowly, concentrating, and then reached my right hand for the back of one of the wooden chairs. I misjudged and stumbled. I was so embarrassed. I knew this house. I moved into this house right after I was born. I couldn't figure out what was wrong with me.

"It's okay. Don't be alarmed." She was so kind and patient. She told me to try again. I did. I grabbed hold of the back of the wooden chair and used it to guide me. It led me to a round waxed wooden seat. So I sat. "How are you feeling, Hope?" She asked.

"I feel a little overwhelmed. I've been living here all my life, but today, I feel like I don't know this place at all."

"You're just familiarizing yourself with the aspects of your home you've been ignoring for all these years. You finished school early, right?" Ms. Maverick asked.

"Yes, as soon as I learned Braille, I started reading anything I could get my hands on, literally," I chuckled as I replied. I was pretty good at recalling information, so I was sure getting to know my home better wouldn't be any different. "You've been coming here for a week now, and I know very little about you. You don't have to get personal if you don't want to." Ms. Maverick didn't seem to mind me inquiring.

"I had Diabetic Retinopathy. It is an eye disease," she said.

"So, how do you have sight?" I asked.

"It can be reversible, and in my case, it was. I am 31 now, but when I was 22, I developed this vision disorder. I was blind for a year. For the first month, I felt sorry for myself and let my family take care of me. I am one of three, so my older sister and younger brother took turns making my meals, and my mom helped me bathe and get dressed." She was fighting back tears. She took a long pause. "I was a toddler all over again. I fell into a deep depression, and my parents took me to see a therapist."

She grabbed what I assumed was a tissue out of her purse and wiped her eyes.

"My therapist convinced me that I didn't have to stop living. So, I didn't. I realized blindness was something that happened to my eyes, not me." She stood up in front of me. She looked a little scary because she looked like a ghostly, dark figment. She continued.

"I decided I would still be me despite my blindness. So, I did. And that's what I want for you, Hope. Be you, despite your blindness." I looked up at the intimidating, yet endearing image hovering over me and smiled. She excused herself to go to the bathroom. I stayed at the kitchen table and reflected on her message to me. "Be me despite my blindness"

Ms. Maverick returned from collecting herself, and sat across from me again. "Are you okay?" I asked.

"Yes, it's just hard to think about sometimes," she uttered. I reached out my hand to wrap my finger around her very thin wrist to console her.

"My mother named me Hope because she hoped I would overcome any health challenges that I had to face. After a few years, Daddy started calling me Moon. You see, the moon has its own identity. It's different from everything else in space. Like I am different from everything in my space. It's not a planet, star, or galaxy. It is a natural satellite maneuvering around the world doing its own thing. The moon shines even in darkness like me. So that's what I plan to do: shine through this darkness."

"That's a beautiful story, Moon. So are you!" She said with a smile.

Ms. Maverick continued coming over, day after day, week after week, month after month. She repeated the same teaching as she did in the kitchen and in every room in my house until every inch and crevice became second nature to me. I became so familiar that it almost felt like I could see vividly wherever I was. I started pouring my own milk and making my own peanut butter and jelly sandwiches at night while everyone was asleep. I even made it back to my room without using the wall. Ms. Maverick became part of the family. My Momma invited her over for dinner at least twice a month.

My favorite times with Ms. Maverick were the day outings. She started taking my mother's place as my escort to many of the places I routinely went. She took me to my Physics class on Wednesdays and my Calculus class on Fridays. We went to the mall and my favorite place in all of Washington, D.C., Hains Point. I loved the smell of the Potomac River, especially on misty days.

There was something else different about our outings. My mother drove me everywhere, but Ms. Maverick and I took public transportation. I had only used public transportation once, and that was when I snuck out to the rally with Angel. We caught the subway. Angel and everyone I knew called the train. Ms. Maverick and I caught the bus. For two weeks, she let me feel the silver coins that distinctly differed in size so I would know how much to put in the machine. Silver was always tough for me to see, even with my glasses on. It was better to feel the coins. I knew the penny, though, because of the contrast.

After two weeks of learning the X line, the V line, etc., I was ready to try traveling on my own. Momma was so worried the first couple of times that I went out alone. Ms. Maverick had to stay at my house for the whole day, consoling her until I made it back safely each time. She finally got to the point where she could kiss me goodbye without hesitation as long as I told her where I was going and when I'd be back, but I knew she was praying whenever I left the house. Poor Momma, she was such a worry-wart.

CHAPTER FOURTEEN

Part I
"Love"

"No sooner met but they looked, no sooner looked but they loved, no sooner loved but they sighed, no sooner sighed but they asked one another the reason, no sooner knew the reason, but they sought the remedy; and in these degrees have they made a pair of stairs to marriage."

William Shakespeare, As You Like It

After completing the coaching sessions, I had a newfound confidence. My mother used to drag me out of bed two hours early to help me get ready for school or the day. After coaching, the big fluorescent green numbers on my alarm clock flashed and woke me up bright and early at seven, not six. Any chance I got to spend at Hains Point, I took it. On non-school days, I was always there with the mid-morning joggers. I sat on the third bench from the right. No one was ever sitting there. It was like that seat was reserved for me. Every day I would sit there for two hours at least, looking out at the Potomac as it looked back at me. I took deep breaths as it threw its mist at me and allowed me to take in its fresh air scent. We established an unspoken codependence. I gave it an audience, and it gave me peace.

One day, as the river and I engaged in our usual banter, a familiar scent sat next to me. I would've been scared if it had been unfamiliar, but it was an old acquaintance. It was the scent of Lagerfeld cologne. This time it didn't smell as good. It was mixed with sweat, but I didn't mind. It wasn't awful. I could feel his body heat. It felt weird! It wasn't my Daddy checking on me to see if I was okay. It was a different feeling. It wasn't a feeling of security. This feeling was very very unfamiliar but I really liked it.

He didn't even say anything. I wasn't sure if he was checking me out because without peripheral vision, I couldn't tell if he was checking me out, but I hoped he was. I hoped he was the strong rally guy who smelled like Lagerfeld, but I wasn't sure. I couldn't see, and I was too excited to turn to my left. Not to mention, I didn't want him to think he was all that if you know what I mean. Angel told me a guy should never know how much you like him because if he became too confident he would start flexing on you. That meant taking you for granted and treating you like you didn't matter. The whole time, though, I imagined myself laying my head on his masculine shoulder while enjoying a picnic on the grass and taking in the smells and sounds of the river. I wanted to kiss him too.

We sat. Both of us were mesmerized by each other's presence. I wanted to turn and say something, but damn! I didn't know if it was him or not. What if I had turned around and said hi to a stranger? Worse than that, what if he was a grown old man? Ugh, I thought. I kept looking out at the calm water and gray sky. He got up. He was so tall! I could see his tall shadow hovering over me, but I didn't look up. I was too nervous. I didn't acknowledge him. He reached down and used his finger to lift up my chin. His face was somewhat of a blur. I could make out enough handsome to be excited. Yes, my suspicion was right. It was that handsome face and brown eyes that rescued me at the rally. He finally did it. He squatted down once my smile gave him permission to.

"Hi," he said.

"Hi," I said. There were so many butterflies all over my body, even my toes. I could only see a figment of his fineness. I was very confident that he was probably so much finer through clear eyes. That's okay. I thought that seeing some fine was better than seeing no fine at all.

"I remember you from the rally at DCU a couple of months ago," he said.

"Are you sure it was me?" I said.

"There was nobody else there more beautiful," he said. I blushed. I didn't even know him, and I wanted to kiss him.

"Well, aren't you a smooth talker?" I said.

"I'm only telling the truth," he said. Suddenly, the sounds of the river, birds flying and chirping, and cars driving by at a distance all went quiet. I couldn't hear a thing. I only heard the beat of my heart thumping through my hoodie. I didn't know what to say. I couldn't stop smiling.

"You have a beautiful smile, too," he said. I kept blushing.

"Hey Nehemiah, you're still riding with me, man?" A voice yelled in our direction from a distance.

"Yes, Marshall, man, give me a second," replied Nehemiah.

"Can I see you again?" I didn't hesitate or play hard to get at all.

"Yes," I said.

CHAPTER FOURTEEN

Part II
"Hope and Nehemiah"

"Love is patient. Love is Kind"

1 Corinthians 13:4-8

My favorite flower was the Yellow Daisy. Nehemiah had four tied together with a yellow ribbon taped to the outside of my window every morning when he came to pick me up. He was so romantic like that. We drove to Hains Point together on the days I didn't have class. He had to stay fit during basketball season. When we arrived at the park, Nehemiah scurried into the parking lot and parked his 300ZX. He got out of the car and opened the door for me. I felt like Cinderella; well, before the clock struck twelve. I offered him my hand, and he guided me to my favorite spot. He leaned down, kissed me on my cheek, and said, "I won't be long, baby, okay?"

"Okay," I replied, blushing and smiling. While he jogged, squatted, and crunched, I took in the river's surroundings. I smelled and heard everything: Nehemiah's sweat and Lagerfeld, other morning joggers passing by, birds that hit the water like skipped rocks, sending mist into the air, chirping, and calling to one another, fumes from random fishing boats sounding their horns, the morning dew on wet, freshly cut grass, and my own Dove soap and baby lotion. I tried watching Nehemiah run, but he was a blur; a nice blur, but still a blur. One that I couldn't stop thinking about. I thought about the ways that he made me laugh all the time.

Although, I thought monkeys were adorable and funny too. Their sounds were hilarious, especially when imitated by Nehemiah. He was so cute! He always tried to cheer me up whenever I got frustrated because I couldn't see something clearly or I missed a step.

"Where's that smile? Where's that smile?" He would say. If I didn't smile at him, he would get close to my face and start his monkey song. That song made me laugh every time. It never failed. I always ended up laughing hysterically and sometimes needing a bathroom visit afterwards.

"Boo!"

"Hey, stop that," I said, startled and annoyed by how sweaty he was.

"Don't you want a hug from your man?" His sweaty armpits got close to my nose.

"Ewww, stop it," I giggled. He sat next to me, chugging down the water in his thermos.

"You ready to go, baby?" I took a deep breath, taking in the morning smells one more time. I choked a little. Nehemiah was a little smelly. He laughed.

"Yes, I'm ready." He reached out his hand like the perfect gentleman he always was, and I gladly extended my hand. We always walked slowly, but like a regular couple, not like I was a cripple with a guide dog. Nehemiah knew that I could see a little, so as long as we took it slow, we enjoyed a sweet and intimate walk while our clasped hands swung back and forth. The movement had a rhythm. It was like we were dancing. One that was a little familiar. I remembered having a similar dance with Angel when we were younger. It was especially nice when there were no steps to climb or curbs to maneuver. Nehemiah was becoming my friend, like Angel but different, way different. My whole body tingled inside and out whenever he was near me. Angel didn't have that effect on me. Nehemiah was becoming so much more than a best friend and I liked it.

"So, what do you want to do today?" Nehemiah asked.

"Don't you have b-ball practice today?"

"Yeah, but I should be done by three,"

"I have class at two, so that's perfect."

"Oh Damn!"

"What?" I inquired.

" I have a game tonight. Maybe you can hangout after!" He stated with excitement.

"I'm not sure. I'll let you know."

Nehemiah got me home in a flash. I still hadn't got the hang of using my key to open the door yet, so Nehemiah walked me to the door and rang the doorbell.

He leaned in. It surprised me. We hadn't kissed on the lips yet, and we had been hanging out for a month. I licked my lips in preparation and as soon as his breath got closer, my mother opened the door. If I were handing out awards, she would receive the bad timing award for sure. Why didn't she look out the peephole? He got scared and kissed me on the forehead, thanks to Ms. Pranita Nosey!

"I'll see you after class at 3:15," he said, reminding me.

"Okay, have fun at practice," I said with both a smile and a frown of agitation all wrapped up into one.

"Hi, Moon," Mom uttered. I looked at her with disgust and embarrassment.

"Hi, Moon? Is that all you have to say?" I retorted.

"What do you mean?" Mom inquired.

"What do you mean? What do I mean? Why didn't you just excuse yourself, Momma, when you saw him leaning in to kiss me?"

"Moon, I did not see him leaning in. I didn't know what was going on. I was answering the damn door because the doorbell rang," she said, frustrated and annoyed.

"Well, when you saw it was Nehemiah and me, why didn't you leave? You stood there watching and waiting for me. I know my way around this house, Momma, and I know my way around most places now. I no longer need an escort. Please respect my privacy," I declared. The house was a little dim, so I counted the 200 steps it took to get to my room door. I opened the door, stepped in, and slammed it shut behind me. I sat on my bed, looking at the images of my civil rights timeline, and fell asleep. I was awakened by my mother calling my name.

"Hope!" She yelled.

"Yes, Momma?"

"Nehemiah is on the phone." Once she heard, "May I speak to Hope" and then my voice, she hung up. She better had, I thought. Nehemiah had a really low baritone voice. I loved it. Even without him in front of me, it sent chills down my spine. His voice entranced me.

"Hi," he said.

"Hi," I said with a really big smile.

"What's up? I have a break for ten minutes."

"Oh, I didn't know your coach gave you guys that long of a break."

"Yea, he does. He's working us hard today for some reason. I guess because we play GW this week. Are you going to come to my game tonight against Bowen? It's at DCU."

"Yes, of course," I said.

"Great. I just wanted to hear your voice. I have to go. Marshall is calling me to return to practice. See you soon, Moon."

I blushed. I would usually object to anybody but my parents and Ms. Maverick calling me that, but Nehemiah was special. I smiled the biggest flirtiest smile and said sweetly and softly, "Goodbye." I hung up the phone, continued smiling, and dove face-first into my full-size bed and lime green pillows. I wanted tonight's game to hurry up and come. I immediately called Angel.

Ringgggggg! Ringgggggg! Ringgggggg! The phone rang forever.

"Hello?" Angel answered, sounding sleepy and annoyed.

"Girl, it's me. Why do you sound all sleepy? It's noon."

"I had a Physics exam this morning. I was up studying all night. Why do you sound all happy in the middle of the day?"

"I think I'm falling in love with Nehemiah."

"In love! You've only been hanging out with him for one month. Calm down, Hope."

"Jealousy is a horrible condition, Ms. Womack. You'll find love as good as this someday. Angel, seriously, he brings me my favorite flowers."

"Awwww. That's sweet," she said sarcastically.

"What's the problem?" I asked.

"Nothing. That was sweet, but I don't trust him yet," Angel retorted with her usual sassiness.

"His friend Marshall is so cute, not cuter than Nehemiah, but cute."

"No offense, but how do you know he's so cute? I thought you saw him once from a distance without your glasses when he picked up Nehemiah from the park. I know your sight is getting a little stronger, but you did not get close enough to see how cute he is."

"Okay, Okay you caught me. I did see broad shoulders and a tall shadow. Come on, Angel Pleassssse!" I begged.

Pleasssse, what?"

"Please go to the DCU game tonight!"

"Hope, you know how much I hate sports," she said with agitation in her voice.

My family has always protected me, but Angel was by far the most protective. She was my very beautiful and sassy bodyguard.

"Well, tonight is your chance to get to know him and maybe even meet Marshall," I said excitedly.

"I'll pass," she sighed.

"Angel, c'mon. Don't make me sit on those bleachers all alone."

"Try harder," she said jokingly.

"I have heard girls at DCU say that Marshall looks like Allen Payne from *New Jack City*."

"Oooooooo! I'm sold. I'll be there," Angel said enthusiastically.

"Yes, you're my girl. Thank you," I took a deep sigh. I think my insides were dancing inside.

"We're going to look so good, and I'm taking you there two hours early so you can count steps and become familiar with the gym," Angel said.

"Bet, good plan! Come over early to help me pick out a cute outfit." I demanded.

"Okay, you know I got you. Bye."

Angel hung up and was at my room door three hours later with a Bantu cream relaxer, blow dryer, and flat iron. My natural curly Afro was turned into a straight shoulder-length bob in no time. She even put mascara and lip gloss on me. Even with my glasses on, I was all that and a bag a chip, and so was Angel. We were both obsessed with Chili, Left Eye, and T-Boz from TLC and our other favorite girl group was Xscape. I rocked a denim jumper with a florescent yellow bandeau, and Angel flaunted the classic girl group look with the baggy camo pants and a fitted black baby T-top. We were ready two hours early, just like she had planned.

The Sports Center smelled of sports equipment and floor wax. My big Coach bucket bag around my neck hung diagonally across me, making my neck a little sweaty, or Maybe it's because I was on step 282. Counting was exhausting, but it helped. I didn't want to look like a helpless cripple after walking in looking so fly. I wanted to represent my man. I started counting from the subway station exit. Angel knew not to bother me. I told her when I would start counting.

"283, 84, 85... I whispered as I reached the front bleacher where Nehemiah said he would leave some sports equipment to save us a seat.

"86, 87..." Angel cut me off.

"You finished yet? I'm hungry. Let's go get a burger." I rolled my eyes. She was so lucky I only had two more numbers to count, or it would've gotten ugly.

"Hope, come on. I'm hungry." Angel repeated. When we returned to the Sports Center, balls were bouncing off the glass backboards as strong, long, white, tan, and brown muscular legs squatted to take a position to shoot in preparation for the game. The blurs of players jogging back and forth down the long shiny court started to form a rhythm. I wished I could see Nehemiah a little clearer, but I saw the big red number 25 on the back of his gold jersey. His curly locks looked fuzzy from, but I knew how they felt, just like silk, so It didn't matter. Angel kept nudging me, talking about the girls checking out our outfits and hairdos. I didn't care. I was too busy admiring my Nehemiah. He finally spotted me and waved. I waved back with a big blushing smile. Angel waved too.

"Girl, he is fine," she said, smacking my shoulder.

"Ouch! stop hitting me, Angel. That hurts, and I know, isn't he? I think I'm in love," I said, blushing.

"Shut up, Hope. Too soon," she retorted. I rolled my eyes at her again. I was annoyed. I wanted her to stop saying that. I knew how I felt. "What number is Marshall? Fine brothers stick together, so I know he's cute, too," she inquired and declared.

"Marshall is number 31. His last name is Ferguson. He has dreadlocks, I think. They could be braids. You tell me when you spot him. Girl, I don't pay attention to Marshall. Nehemiah is the only man I need to focus on," I said with sass.

"Oh, I see him. Oooooooo. Very cute. Is he white?"

"I'm not sure. I think he might be mixed. I think Nehemiah said his father is White, and his mother is Black.

"That's interesting. What if he doesn't like me?" Angel said with worry.

"What's not to like? You are a satin doll. That's what my mom calls you when you're not around. How could he not like your cumin, flawless skin, and your, as you often refer to fly overtones? Oh, don't worry, girlfriend. He's going to like what he sees." I stated confidently.

"Oh, God! He's looking over here!" Angel stated nervously.

Buzzzzz! The buzzer went off. Marshall made something happen that I didn't understand. I think it's because he was checking out Angel and should have been paying attention to the game.

"I think it's safe to say that he likes what he sees," I said. Angel blushed.

CHAPTER FOURTEEN

Part III
"More Justice and Less Nehemiah"

"Injustice anywhere is a threat to justice everywhere."

Dr. Martin Luther King Jr.

The Black Student Alliance was a campus group formed during the sixties to provide a platform where like-minded Black students could assemble and speak their truth about any current controversial topic in society. It provided a safe space to prepare rallies, design petitions, video speeches, or compose letters of protest to our government. The group was usually pretty small unless there was something really big going on in the world that we wanted to change. It was open to anybody, although only Black students participated in the meetings, and it was usually the same familiar faces.

After my unofficial liberation from all of my bodyguards, I started catching the train to school to participate in the BSA meetings taking place in response to the Rodney King verdict. I was still kind of shy, though. I didn't have much to say. I was more of a reactor, not an initiator. I usually just listened to what everyone else had to say, even though thoughts burned inside me like lava. I had opinions and ideas, but the words wouldn't form or unleash. I guess I just wasn't stimulated enough.

One day our president, Langston Baldwin, addressed us from the podium. The room became silent except for one excited fan, "Alright! Speak! Langston, my brother!" Langston gave him a half smile of appreciation and began.

"Hello, brothers and sisters for the cause. I'm so happy to see so many of your smiling faces. I stand here today with a wedge of grief in my heart for Brother Rodney, and I know we can do more."

"Yes, we can!" a girl screamed from the back of the room.

"I hear you back there, sister!" Langston replied, extending his right arm straight up in the air with his fist clenched tight. That's what black activists did as a sign of solidarity. He continued:

"I have watched that video over and over again, intentionally. I never want to forget the brutality brother Rodney endured. The last time I viewed it, I envisioned myself on the ground. I was there, brothers and sisters being beaten excessively. That was me on the ground being kicked and punched. That was you on the ground. That was my father on the ground, his father, and his father before him, and it must stop. We cannot stand here watching this country validate police brutality against African Americans. That is what that verdict did. It justified the crime. It said the senseless beating of black men and women by our police force is right. It said It is fair. It must go on, and Black lives are not deemed important. It says to beat them. Lynch them. Hate them.

Sisters and brothers of the BSA, we are small but mighty. There are ways to reach the decision-makers in this society without risking our lives. We're here at this university to better position ourselves within this country's workforce as theologians, doctors, lawyers, business owners, etcetera. We are not here to make a difference using radical methods that might harm innocent people. We want change and to be heard! That is all."

His voice and words maintained such rhythmic eloquence. He was an orchestra of change, and we were captivated by his instruments. Listening to Brother Baldwin made me want to take action, but I didn't. I wanted to get up and shout a phrase of agreement like others did during his speech, but I didn't. I continued to listen with immeasurable admiration. I felt so unconfident for some reason. I stretched out my legs in front of me, careful not to kick the person's chair. The cafeteria-like fluorescent lights permitted my eyes to slightly see the brown and beige faces that decorated the small drafty room. It was usually used as a classroom for the Math department. This was great for me because I was very familiar with the buildings used by the School of Mathematics. Nehemiah was starting to know them well too. He was a Biology major, but he met me between classes sometimes. He was supposed to come to this meeting after basketball practice. Langston coughed and took a sip of water from his cup and then continued,

"I had a thought last night. I dreamed about it. We've marched. We've petitioned, don't misunderstand me; those are great steps in the direction towards making a change, however,

we need to face the lions head-on. We need to hold our policymakers accountable, so I have decided to go to Capitol Hill and demand change."

Suddenly, there was a loud roar! A voice rang out.

"That's exactly what we need to do, Brother Langston!" Another voice rang out.

"Let's do it! Let's organize a rally right on the steps of Congress!" said one more voice.

Langston interrupted.

"That's not quite what I had in mind. As some of you may know, my father is a judge, which is where I think my thirst for justice derived. I spoke with my father this morning, and he told me he could pull a few strings to get me in to address Congress. I can attend a congressional meeting and share the need for change. He said he thinks he can get one other person in along with me. Do I have any volunteers?" Langston asked with a sense of urgency in his voice.

Nehemiah walked in just as Langston called for volunteers. The room became surprisingly silent. I heard Neha's footsteps outside the door, that was my new nickname I gave him, and the slow and subtle opening of the door. I stood up excitedly to inform him of my whereabouts. Langston misinterpreted my actions.

"Hope! Great, my sister! I am so happy you have accepted this brave challenge. Everyone stand up and give Ms. Hope Neilson the fist of peace." Nehemiah approached the corner where my chair was located, and we greeted each other with stunned eyes. Everyone stood up. The room was painted with a portrait of brown and beige arms raised high—all except Nehemiah's and mine. My heart stopped for a moment, and then it started beating again but really fast. I looked down to locate my collapsed symbol stick. Neha picked it up for me. I assembled it and reached for Neha's hand, silently asking his permission to accompany me to the front. Instead of agreeing, he took my hand, kissed the inside of it, and then directed my hand toward the podium to go alone. I looked up at his blurry eyes and observed his sudden posture. His arm was now raised in peace.

I allowed my stick to lead me to the front. I smiled at Langston's fuzzy goatee and circular-shaped dark eyes. I turned to face the now large crowd of arms and smiles. My body was partially paralyzed with fear. I took a deep breath, raised my right arm hesitantly, and formed the fist of peace in agreement.

CHAPTER FIFTEEN

"Becoming Courageous"

"It takes courage to grow up and become who you really are."

E.E. Cummings

Nehemiah dropped me off in front of my house like he always did. Usually, I would sit in the car for a few minutes and make plans for our next date, but I was still consumed with what just happened at the BSA meeting, so I kissed him goodbye and went inside.

Momma was sitting at the kitchen table reading the paper. I could hear Benny and Bailey playing with their train set in their room. My plate of food was sitting on the table on my green place mat with the fork and knife rolled up in a yellow paper napkin.

"Hi, Momma."

"Hi, Moon. How was the meeting?" She inquired, smiling with approval.

"It was fine," I mumbled.

"You okay, baby?"

"Yes, I'm fine."

"Okay, well, eat your dinner. I'm going to sit here for a little while and read the paper."

"Okay." I was so consumed with the thought of addressing Congress, I could barely eat, and it was Momma's famous five-cheese lasagna. I put large chunks on my fork, anticipating satisfying my major hunger pains, but I only took small bites. Momma glanced from behind her Washington Post and spied my half-full plate. She immediately stopped reading, folded the paper in four large folds, and sighed.

"Moon, I'm going to ask you one more time. What is wrong with you? You're acting like the wind has been knocked right out of you."

"Momma, I agreed to do something I am not ready for."

"What is it, baby?"

"Langston, our president's father, pulled some strings to get us in to address Congress about creating stiffer accountability policies for law enforcement agencies that misuse their authority."

"That's wonderful, Moon! What's wrong with that? That's a wonderful opportunity. Something legal certainly needs to be put in place," she said.

"I know, but...," I stuttered as I lost my train of thought.

"But what, Moon? Spit it out," Momma retorted with frustration and impatience.

"He could only get one person to accompany him to Capitol Hill. He asked for volunteers, and everyone got really scared and didn't volunteer. I stood up to greet Neha, and Langston mistook that as a yes. Momma, I don't know what to do. I don't want to go with him." My heart started pounding the way that it did at the BSA meeting.

"What are you afraid of, Moon?" She asked endearingly.

"I don't know," I mumbled.

"You know. It's the same thing that stood in your way the first time you crossed the street by yourself. The same fear took you almost a year to spend the day at Angel's house. She took a deep breath and continued. "Moon, you need to get out of your way, baby."

"What do you mean?" I inquired confusingly.

"I mean, stop thinking that you're going to fail or that you're not enough. Nielsen is my married name. You have Keen' blood running through your veins. Your father knew good and well what he was getting when he married Ms. Pranita Keen, and I want you to know who you are. We are strong, intelligent and courageous people," Momma said as she leaned across the table and scooped my chin up with her tan pointer finger. She softly kissed my forehead. Then she got up, took the folded newspaper off the table, and went to her room like she did every evening after dinner.

Once I heard her door click closed, I took a moment to think about this inner strength. She once told me how she and Aunt Addie attended the March on Washington. She shared how they worked tirelessly to make signs; they were only nine and fourteen when the March occurred. She shared that it was a hot

August day, but she, her siblings, and Grandma Keen' walked miles in the heat to fight for civil rights. After a long three days of reflection, I was ready.

The US Capitol looked like a large church cathedral. As I walked, I hoped that the Lord would take away the knots that consumed the bottom of my stomach. As I approached the top of the last flight of cement stairs, the knots got worse.

The old wooden door was heavy. When I entered, the openness created by the lofty ceilings and fat, tall poles reminded me of the museums I sometimes visited with my family. I felt like I was in OZ. Although I couldn't clearly see the historic images painted on the ceilings, the gold floors sparkled so luminously under my feet, so I couldn't help but appreciate the room's radiance.

The foyer outside the room where the congressional committee met was becoming larger and larger. Langston told me to meet him there. I waited for a few minutes until suddenly I felt a large masculine hand clasping mine. I looked up, and it was Langston. His figment was always tall, but being so close made him a giant. Langston was a dark, smoothed-skinned guy with a mustache that made him look older than a college junior. His khakis fit him neatly along with his dark blue button-down oxford shirt and blue or black bowtie, I couldn't make out which color. He wore goggle-looking glasses like me. I hoped mine made me look as smart as his made him. We walked in and were directed by a well-dressed White lady. She told us to walk toward the long brown wooden table. As I walked, my legs became increasingly heavy. I finally dragged my legs down the narrow walkway and eventually came upon neatly placed suited bodies on each side of me. I finally approached the table, Langston pulled out a chair for me, and I sat. We sat facing the rows of wooden desks and microphones purposely placed in front of the American flag.

When permitted to speak, Langston did just that. He was fearless and eloquent, as usual. I listened to his harmonious song with so much admiration. He sang of a new day of real visible equal rights for Black and brown Americans. He sang about the need for legislation to protect Black men who consistently fall victim to excessive force by police. I smiled subtly, taking in every note of his harmonious plea. Suddenly, his song ended with, "Thank you, honorable Congresswoman Holmes-Norton." My smile stopped as it was replaced with a large lump of nervousness in my throat. I was given the go-ahead to address the committee. Langston gently tapped my tense fist as it rested on the shiny wooden table.

I went into my bag and took out the large manilla folder that housed my speech. I took a deep breath, and before I knew it, I started my song.

"Dear honorable congressional committee." I cleared my throat multiple times and finally gave a loud hum! Hum! Into my fisted hand. I paused, allowing the rows of stares to numb me. I sat frozen for eight seconds. I could hear the clicking of the large wooden whining wall clock in the back of the room annoyingly going, one click, two clicks, three clicks, four clicks, five, six, seven, eight.

"Your statement, Ms. Neilson," Congresswoman Holmes-Norton stated, agitated with my delay.

"I'm sorry, ma'am," I began.

"Dear honorable congressional committee, the constitution guarantees freedoms to all Americans, not just a select majority. We are all entitled to the protection granted by this doctrine. Unfortunately, Black men repeatedly fall short." I continued, and my volume increased as my confidence surged. *"They have been victims of police brutality for decades. This country has cheated the Black man. Where are their inalienable rights? When is this governmental body going to create a law that explicitly enforces protection from the evils of excessive force used by our law enforcement agencies that have terrorized generations of Black people for many years? I am here to demand change. I demand change that looks like a law that guarantees stiffer penalties for police officers that use excessive force. I demand change that provides training for police officers designed to protect our communities from police brutality. I demand change that looks like more police officers who look like me working in our communities. Change is overdue, and it can't happen without your help. Thank you for your time, honorable committee."*

CHAPTER SIXTEEN

"The After Party"

The Firebirds beat Bowen State, and Marshall invited a bunch of us over to his house for a party. Marshall and Nehemiah graduated from Banneker Institute together. The kids at Banneker were really smart. If you attended Banneker, you were considered a Banneker Scholar. That's another one of Nehemiah's many qualities that I loved. He was so intelligent. I think he was even smarter than me. Well, that might still be out for the jury to decide. I scored higher than him on the SAT. I scored a 1500, and he scored 1450. He really struggled with that academic triumph I had over him. They were also really wealthy. They lived in the wealthy Chevy community. Marshall and Nehemiah's neighbors were Washington Redskin players, senators, and congressmen. One of the Redskins lived directly across the street from Marshall. When my Momma would tell me stories about Chevy, she referred to the neighborhood as upper crust. She said it was the Beverly Hills of D.C.

After the game, Angel and I remained seated, waiting for Nehemiah and Marshall to meet us. My hearing became increasingly hyper-sensitive over the years, so I could hear all of their remarks. Two girls with long braids stepped off the bleachers as they passed me. One of them said, "That's the blind girl that hooked up with Nehemiah." The other one immediately said, "What?"

Another pair walked up to Angel and I while we were seated. I had on my glasses, but it didn't matter because I was still cute, so I confidently looked up with inquiring eyes. They were dressed in cut-off shorts, sweat hoodies, and Timberland boots. The one who spoke to me had the lightest, most beautiful porcelain skin. She was wearing a purplish color lipstick and I think a nose ring. She was smacking on her chewing gum so obnoxiously when she addressed Angel. "Which one of ya'll is dating Nehemiah?" She said as she went back to smacking and popping her gum. I looked her up and down before I answered,

"Me."

"Oh, well, I'm his ex, but I want you to know that it's not really over, so don't get comfortable in my space," she retorted. Angel stood up to address them both.

"Get out of her face, girl."

"I'm not in her face, and if I was, how would she know? Can she even see me?" She said.

"She can see you. I can see you. How can we miss all of that ugly? She is sitting here minding her business, and because you can't handle Nehemiah moving on, you want to come and start trouble. Get away from here and deal with the fact that he doesn't want your ugly anymore," Angel retorted.

"Yvette, stop," the other girl said.

"Yea, Yvette, stop before we call security. I look too good to be fighting you over some man that doesn't want you," said Angel. For the first time in my life, I stayed seated and was glad to be legally blind. I could barely see her, so I tuned her out as best as I could. I looked straight ahead, concentrating on the figures across the Sports Center. I think it was people coming into the other exit doors on the opposite end of the Sports Center because the figments were moving toward a bright red light, which usually meant exit. Suddenly the figments behind the people going toward the exit doors were moving closer to us. As they got closer and closer, I could see two tall contrasting figures. One was dark, and the other was light. They both were carrying duffle bags and wearing red Firebird hoodies. The darker figure got really close, and I smelled the Lagerfeld. His curly locks were bushy and tickling the top of my head. Suddenly he did the unthinkable. He kissed me on the lips right in front of Yvette. I could still hear her nearby. Angel bursted into uncontrollable laughter. Yvette and her friend grunted with agitation and left. I felt victorious. It felt nice to have a boyfriend. I smiled.

"What's that beautiful smile for?" Nehemiah asked.

"Nothing much," I said.

"You ready to go?" Nehemiah asked.

"Yes, but wait. Marshall, this is my best friend Angel," I said.

"Nice to meet you," he said.

Angel waved hello, and said, "Nice to meet you too."

"Is it nice to meet me?" Marshall flirtatiously inquired. Guys went for Angel mostly because of her long eyelashes. Even I could see those things. She also had dimples. Our friends in the neighborhood often called her Dimples instead of Angel. I I was pretty sure the dimples and eyelashes captivated him like they did most guys.

"I guess," replied Angel, playing hard to get.

"What do you mean, you guess?" Marshall replied on the prowl.

"It's nice to meet you, Marshall," Angel blushed.

"That's better," he said. Marshall pulled up the falling duffle bag and placed it back onto his shoulders. "I'm starving. Neha, meet me at my house. The party starts in an hour." He looked Angel up and down like she was an inviting dish of almond-flavored ice cream. "They are coming to my house. Do you want to ride with me so we can get to know each other?"

"No thanks, Mr. Marshall. I can get to know you plenty riding with Hope and Nehemiah and seeing you an hour from now," Angel responded with a flirtatious undertone. Marshall smiled. Basketball players weren't used to working to get a girl, but Angel wasn't just any girl.

I latched onto Nehemiah's tight, muscular arm like I had won the prize. I didn't have my symbol stick, so I let Neha be my guide. It wasn't as embarrassing as I thought it would be with him leading me out because it was like I was a princess being escorted by a handsome prince, and I was the envy of all, especially Yvette.

When we got to his car, he helped me as usual, but this time he picked me up and placed me in the seat. I laughed as he carried me. It really felt like I was in some fairytale.

Neha got in the car, put on his seatbelt, leaned over to clamp my seatbelt, and gave me one more passionate kiss on the lips. He knew that I was perfectly capable of fastening my own seatbelt, but he told me it gave him an excuse to be closer to me. I was extremely flattered, of course.

Das Efx started projecting from the tape cassette, "Microphone Check, Mica, Microphone Checka...."

"Turn that up!" Angel said. She was in the back singing the song, snapping her fingers and nodding her head to every lyric.

"*Riggidy-raow, Ziggidy Gadzuks, Here I go, so*

Fliggedy-flame on, g-geronimo, yo

I biggedy-burn riggedy-rubber when I blabber great

I miggedy-make the Wonder Twins deactivate," *she* sang before her voice faded out of our focus.

"Why was Yvette talking to you? What did she want?" Nehemiah inquired. My mood went sour. I knew little about her, but I didn't like her.

I sighed heavily and said, "Why do you care? Is there still something going on between you two?"

"NO!" Nehemiah stated reassuringly. "No way. You never have to worry about her. It is over, Hope." He squeezed my hands firmly. I guess he was thinking I was going to break up with him. He stopped at a light and turned to look at me. I didn't have peripheral vision, so the only way that I knew he turned to look at me was when he placed his finger under my chin and turned my face towards him. He looked me in the eyes. "Do you hear me? You are the only girl I want. You and only you." Angel stopped singing. She thought Neha was getting aggressive.

"What's going on?" She inquired abruptly.

"Nothing," I said. I didn't want to get Angel riled up.

"Do you hear me, Moon?" Nehemiah asked repeatedly. My stronger eye released a tear.

"Yes, Neha, I heard you, and I believe you," I stated reassuring him. The light changed, so we didn't kiss in agreement like we wanted to, but we understood.

CHAPTER SEVENTEEN

"Having it All"

"Without human decency and kindness, having it all means absolutely nothing"

Keshia LaVett

I used Neha's car phone to call my mother and tell her I was okay. She answered on the first ring.

"Hi, Momma," I said calmly.

"Hope, where are you? I was expecting you back after the game. It's 11:00. Are you okay?" She inquired urgently.

"Momma, calm down. I'm fine." Nehemiah gently placed his hand on mine and gave it a light squeeze. He was sweet like that. I think it was his way of reassuring me that I was correct. As long as I was with him, I was just fine.

"Well, you could've called me sooner than 11:00 at night to tell me that you are fine. You are not like everyone else, Hope. You are my special baby girl, and I worry," She said with a stifling lump in her throat.

"I know, Momma. I'm sorry to worry you, but I'm not a baby anymore. I'm seventeen and in college," I said. Her voice was engulfed with anger and volume.

"You are still under my roof, Alexandra," she said with an angry tone. She only called me that when she was really agitated with me.

"You will respect my rules," she demanded.

"What rules? You've never told me about any stupid rules," I retorted.

"Watch your tone, Alexandra, before I order you home right now. Stop showing off in front of your friends before I smack the black off of you girl." I got scared. I knew my mother meant business. Smacking the black off of me was not a figure of speech in my house, so I quickly changed my tone and became respectful and apologetic Hope again.

"Yes, Momma. I'm sorry. You didn't tell me what the rules are, so what time should I be home?" I said calmly and politely. She also quickly transformed.

"I guess one is fine. I'll leave the lights on in the hall and kitchen for you. Be very careful, Moon," she said. She called me Moon. That meant she wasn't mad anymore. I sighed with relief, hung up the phone, and turned my head just in time to catch Nehemiah's pleased expression.

"I need to be home by one," I told him.

"Okay," he replied.

"Ms. Pranita, okay?" Angel asked.

"Yeah, she's okay," I said.

"What time do you have to be home?" She asked.

"Apparently, the rule for me is one while I'm living under her roof." Angel laughed.

"Be nice to Ms. Pranita," she suggested jokingly. I waved my hand behind me as my body continued to face the front. My hand gesture spoke for me, saying, I don't care. Angel continued to laugh.

"What time do you have to be in?" I asked.

"Since my seventeenth birthday, it's just been an unspoken understanding. I guess they're just happy I'm home and haven't moved out yet," Angel explained.

"It's also because you're not a cripple," I retorted.

"Stop, Hope. You're not a cripple," she declared.

"She's right; stop calling yourself that," Nehemiah chimed in. I didn't care about their words of encouragement. I knew how my mother made me feel. She still didn't believe in me after all I've been through to become independent, Hope.

I recognized some of the well-lit store signs on Connecticut Avenue as Nehemiah approached his Chevy neighborhood. I had only been in this neighborhood one other time when my mother had to take me to a vision specialist in nearby Georgetown.

Bradley Lane was where Nehemiah and Marshall both lived. They had been friends since kindergarten. They both attended Barneby Academy from Kindergarten through eighth grade and then on to the prestigious Banneker Institute. They both played basketball for Banneker and received athletic scholarships to the District of Columbia University, DCU. Both of them were so fine, although Nehemiah looked better even in a blur. Nehemiah was tall and covered from head to toe in pure brown satin skin. I always told him how much I loved his hair every chance I got. It smelled like fresh citrus all the time. He'd laugh and explain that he and his Jamaican cousins looked alike.

"I'm an Island boy," he said whenever I complimented him on his powerful locks.

We finally drove up to the huge red brick castle of a house. Marshall's car was parked in the driveway of the house. There didn't seem to be other cars parked in the driveway other than Nehemiah's, so I had assumed that all the other people parked on the street or caught the subway. After Nehemiah opened the car door for us, Angel grabbed my hand to walk me in. Nehemiah greeted Marshall on the long rectangular porch as the Poor Righteous Teachers' song "Rock this Funky Joint" rang out from the front door and the many open windows facing the front of the house. Once we got in, I heard a voice direct us to the breakfast room. The breakfast room? How many other special rooms do they have in this place? I asked with admiration.

"They are so rich," Angel said.

"Do we look like we fit? Do we look good compared to everyone else?" I inquired.

"Yes, I'm just jealous. This neighborhood made the one-floor ramblers of *The Stone Community* look extremely small," she said. I laughed.

"Angel, you ain't right, girl. Remember, we're rich in spirit and good looks. Where is my man?" I inquired.

"He is talking to sexy Marshall, but guess who else is in there?" She answered.

CHAPTER EIGHTEEN

"Being Me"

"When you're different, sometimes you don't see the millions of people who accept you for what you are. All you notice is the person who doesn't."

Jodi Picoult

Angel said Marshall was wearing baggy Gap jeans with fresh bubble gum sole Timberland boots and a DCU Firebirds' hoodie. He was the picture of college boy perfection. We hurriedly approached the huddle of Marshall, Neha, Yvette, and, as Angel put it, "her rat-faced friend, Rochelle." It was pretty dark in the house, so Angel guided me to the group and purposely placed me up against Nehemiah, who was leaning on the arm of a piece of furniture. She wanted to make sure that Yvette knew whose man Nehemiah was. I wasn't sure if it was a chair or a sofa. Whatever it was, I bet it was expensive. Nehemiah was holding out his hand to receive me. I felt like a baby being passed from one parent to the other.

He placed me in his arms and squeezed me tightly, and kissed me on my cheek from the back of me. His sweet breath lightly touched my left ear. I wished I could have seen Yvette's face when he did that. I could only imagine the jealousy spewing from her nostrils. I used both of my hands to grab his hands before they went somewhere besides my waist. I knew Nehemiah very well. He leaned in and started whispering the lyrics to the Poor Righteous Teachers song in my ear. The soft air from his whispers tickled my ear, so I laughed, tilting my head to the side away from his lips.

"Hehehehe! Stop," I whispered back, requesting him to refrain but gesturing with my sensual body language to keep going. It was both sweet and flirtatious. The more I laughed, the louder Yvette's voice got. She was babbling about something she and her foolish friends had done the night before. All of a sudden, her voice got louder and closer to where me and Nehemiah were standing.

"Don't you remember how we rode to that stupid club that was closed for renovation?" Yvette said.

"No, I don't remember that girl," laughed her friend. She walked over to Nehemiah and placed her arm on his shoulder, leaning so close to him that I could feel her body heat. I froze. My whole body started to tingle. My heart started racing. It was a fast-moving train.

"Neha, remember when you picked me and Rochelle up and took us to the Metro Club, and it was closed for renovation?" She must have slung those braids of hers because one accidentally hit me on the cheek. I rubbed the area to make sure it didn't leave a mark.

"I was so mad. "Baby, remember?" Her breath was closer to mine. "So, you took us to IHOP to make me feel better. That was so sweet," she purred. Her breath and body got closer. My heart continued racing faster, and I suddenly felt sick. "Remember baby, remember?"

"Get off of me, Yvette. I don't remember," Nehemiah said.

"Ouch! That hurt, Nehemiah. You scratched me. You didn't have to shove. I was going to move," Yvette yelled while rubbing the scratch Nehemiah made on her forearm.

"Hey, watch yourself, Nehemiah. Ever since you got with Helen Keller, you've been acting like you're better than us. You are so lucky we're not back home in Brooklyn. My brothers in New York would teach you a lesson," yelled Rochelle. The music stopped, and the lights came on.

"What's going on?" Marshall inquired. He and Angel came from a remote area. Her red lipstick looked a little smeared. She wore that color to show her school spirit.

"You okay, Hope?" Angel asked.

"Yes, I'm fine. I'm ready to go home, though," I said.

"Everything is fine. That dumb Yvette strikes again," Nehemiah replied frustratingly. I was curious about what he meant by the last part of his statement, but I was ready to go home, so I didn't ask. "Cmon, Moon. I'll take you home."

I was so mad at that girl, but I decided to exit before I stooped to Yvette's trashy level. I started walking as fast as I could. I remembered how many steps I had taken when Angel escorted me to the crowd. The rest I had to figure out with light and blur. I was mad, but I tried to remain calm. I didn't want a repeat of the rally, so anytime I heard, smelled, or saw a human-shaped figment I said excuse me and headed for the cool air that pulled me to the front door. Once I got out the door, I heard my short, fast breaths echoing like microphoned voices. I walked as fast as my legs would allow me. Tears started to stream out of my eyes. I walked and walked until the white wrought iron railing stopped me. Ough! I ran right into it. It Kneed me like an arrow hitting a hunted target. The difference is the edge of the railing was curved, not pointy, so it didn't kill me; it just hurt like hell.

"Damn it!" I yelled. Before I could say another word, Nehemiah rushed up behind me. "Hope, where are you going? I looked all over that house for you. I thought you went into another room. I didn't think you came out here by yourself."

"I'm capable of going places by myself, Neha. I can go anywhere I want without anybody's help," I yelled. I started to walk down the steps. I remembered there were 40 of them. I started counting, "1,2,3,4,5…." Before I reached six, Nehemiah stood in front of me blocking my path. "Move out of my way, Neha," I demanded. He was so tall. I felt like I was being blocked by the actual Monument. He turned around and placed his arms around me by reaching both of his arms towards the back of him. I started smacking the spray-painted picture of Wesley Snipes in New Jack City that was illustrated on the back of his jean jacket. "Get out of my way, Neha. I mean it. Right this minute," I demanded.

"I will if you promise not to walk away. Please, Hope, let me talk to you. Can I, please?" He pleaded with a gentle voice.

"Okay." I sighed and smacked my lips with an attitude as he removed 6'4 inches of height from in front of me. I felt like one of the munchkins from The Wizard of Oz compared to him. If I wasn't so mad, I would have broken into a song. *Follow the yellow brick road.* The Wizard of Oz was one of my favorite movies. Momma used to turn up the brightness on the TV and let me sit close so I could watch and sing along.

I folded my arms in distrust as the wind blew, gently blowing my straightened hair. A strand went in my mouth. It tasted like shampoo and medicine mixed. I thought it must have been all of that product Angel used on my hair before she blow-dried it. I looked up at him, and tried to study him as best as I could. His big head full of hair stole my attention, though. It always did. Neha was such a cool dresser, too. He always had on the latest gear whenever he came to see me unless he was going to work out. Even then, he would wear the latest Nike Air Force One's and Madness sweats. Best of all, he always smelled like Lagerfeld cologne. Mmmmmmm! The appealing scent crept into my nose like an unwanted house guest. I couldn't resist enjoying it, but I didn't smile. It didn't break me down.

"So, what do you have to say, Neha?" I asked.

"What do you want to know?" He responded.

"What are you willing to tell me?" I fired back. It became an empty exchange of questions that got us nowhere.

"I'll tell you anything you want to know, Moon." Nehemiah called me that when he was trying to be sweet.

"I don't want Yvette. I told you that when we were parked in the lot at school."

"Then why does she think you and her are getting back together? Why does she feel comfortable being all over you?" I pushed him. Smoke was blowing out my ears like the mean bull we used to see in cartoons. Tears streamed down my face. I turned to walk away again. He caught the sleeve of my black leather jacket.

"You promised," he said. I stopped. I remembered, so I turned back around, looking down and playing with the zipper on my sleeve.

"I know. I'm still here. Well, what do you have to say, Neha?" I looked up at him with a severe attitude. That smoke that blew out of my ears was now coming out of my nostrils.

"Yvette and I dated for a year last year. I met her last summer while working out at the school gym. We hit it off because our families are from Brooklyn, New York, and we both moved to D.C. when we were babies. I wasn't that serious in the relationship, but she was. I never told her I loved her or anything like that. She just got too serious, so I told her we needed to cool it for a while," he said as his voice and words became mysteriously slow and low, almost whisper-like.

"Why are you being so quiet and nervous all of a sudden? Why did that girl feel comfortable being all over you in that house? You finally pushed her off of you only after you witnessed how uncomfortable it made me. Tell me the truth now, Nehemiah!" I yelled with frustration.

"I don't think I ever really ended it completely. I uh… kinda think we might be still paused."

"What? You mean to tell me you never ended this relationship? No wonder she thinks there is still a chance," I retorted. Suddenly, screams rang out from the house.

"Put me down, Marshall. Put me the hell down. I will rip every inch of her hair out of her head," yelled Angel. Nehemiah and I looked over at the front porch, and Marshall had Angel draped over his right shoulder like a caveman carrying his bride. She was cursing like crazy, wiggling, and kicking her legs like a mermaid because she was wearing a denim skirt. Marshall, out of breath, finally put her down right beside me.

CHAPTER NINETEEN

"Learning How to Forgive"

"Without defeats, how do you really know who the hell you are? If you never had to stand up to something - to get up, to be knocked down, and to get up again - life can walk over you wearing football cleats. But each time you do get up, you're bigger, taller, finer, more beautiful, more kind, more understanding, more loving. Each time you get up, you're more inclusive. More people can stand under your umbrella."

Maya Angelou

"Girl, that was more work than a whole basketball season, including warm-ups." Marshall panted and leaned over resting both hands on his knees.

"Angel, what in the world? Girl, what happened in there?" I inquired.

"Marshall, you alright, man?" Nehemiah asked. Marshall continued to rest his two hands on his knees, hunched over like playing one-on-one defense at a Firebirds' game. He stood up straight to answer.

"Yea, I'm alright. Those girls were in my house flicking off, man! I don't know what was said. After you left to go after Hope, I told Angel to stay put and went to get us both something to drink. When I got back, Angel had Yvette on the floor with both of her hands around her neck. I dropped the cups and ran to grab Angel. I tried prying Angel's skinny little fingers from around her neck, but she wouldn't budge. Finally, Yvette started kicking Angel. She let her neck go after that, and I was able to pull Angel off of her. While Angel was in my arms, Yvette jumped up, smacked Angel in the face, and started pulling her hair. Angel was being pulled out of my arms. I let Angel go so she could defend herself. The next thing I saw was Angel dragging Yvette across my Mom's morning room by her braids, and then Rochelle jumped in it. She tried to attack Angel from behind, so I had to grab her and hold her back while prying Angel's fingers off of Yvette's hair. That went on for a minute, man, and finally, Zack Carter and his brother Vince gave me a hand. Zack held Rochelle back while Vince helped Yvette off the floor. I picked Angel up, flung her over my shoulder, and decided to bring her outside to give us both some air," Marshall finished still kinda out of breath. Sirens rang out from a distance. "Damn! My neighbors must've called. Take them home. I'll handle things here," stated Marshall.

"Are you sure, man?" Nehemiah asked.

"Yeah, I'm good. I'll see you at practice tomorrow." Nehemiah, Angel, and I walked to Neha's car and hurriedly boarded like we were trying to escape a swarm of bees. When we got in the car, Angel started patting down her wild static looking hairs that were darting in all directions. She also had blood coming out of her cheek right on her cheekbone.

"Are you okay, Angel?" I asked. Angel was still angry and worked up.

"That wench is lucky Marshall saved her."

"What happened, Angel?" I asked.

"I don't want to talk about it right now, Hope," she spat angrily. I left her alone after that. I knew how Angel got when she was upset. Whenever she got really upset she would just shut down. Nehemiah tried to comfort me by placing his hand gently on my hand as it rested peacefully on my knee. As soon as it landed, I moved my hand. I could feel his heartbreak. I didn't care at that moment. I just wanted to go home. I wanted to get away from him, and I wanted my Momma.

Nehemiah asked me if I wanted him to walk me to the door when we arrived at my house. I said no. Angel got out first so she could help me. I told her I was fine. I walked up my five brick steps and then along a cement walkway that led to another set of three steps leading to my front door.

"It's just about 2 AM. You didn't make curfew," Angel said as we were walking. When we approached my front door, I heard Neha speed off. Angel rang the doorbell. I don't know why she did that. She knew my brothers and father were asleep. I knew Momma was awake. She opened the door immediately.

"Hi, Momma," I said. I walked to the sofa and sat down after step 25.

"Hi, Ms. Pranita," Angel said, extending her arms to hug Momma.

"Hi, baby," Momma said through gritted teeth. I started to unzip my jacket, and it started before I could get one arm out. My mother's rage was like steam hollering from a hot teapot.

"Do you know what time it is, Hope?" Momma asked. I didn't know if it was a rhetorical question, so I didn't answer. I sat still and stared. Angel remained in the foyer, standing and watching. "I said, DO YOU KNOW WHAT TIME IT IS?" Momma exclaimed.

"I don't know, Momma," I lied. I knew it had to be at least 2:15. I figured if I played dumb, she'd take it easy on me. I also got up and dropped my jacket on the floor, pretending to aim for the brown recliner my Daddy liked to sit in to watch Sunday football. I missed and stumbled. I had to make it look good. It worked. She stopped yelling. She sighed.

"Moon, sit down," she said. I was Moon again. I thanked God. I took a big breath of relief. Momma's voice started to crack. She walked over to sit next to me on the sofa. "Moon."

"Yes, Momma," I answered.

"I'm still getting used to this new independent you. You have a boyfriend now." Momma stated.

"Not for long," I uttered under my breath.

"What?"

"Nothing," I said.

"Well, you are going to parties and school games and wearing makeup. You have gone from my helpless baby needing her mother to pour her milk to this young woman who needs me less and less every day. It's happening too fast, Moon," Momma exclaimed.

"Excuse me, Ms. Pranita?" Angel interrupted.

"Yes, baby?" Momma answered. Before Angel could ask her question, Momma hopped up like a grasshopper and ran over to her. "What happened to your face, Angel?"

"Nothing. I'll be okay. I just need to clean it and get a bandage. That's what I was about to ask for."

"Angel, that doesn't look like nothing. I'm calling your mother right now." Momma said.

"Please don't. I don't want to worry her, and it's so late. I'll be okay. I promise. I just want to clean it and get some sleep. Can I stay over tonight?"

"Yes, of course, baby. Moon, go with her and help her get settled. Angel, promise me you will call your parents in the morning as soon as you wake up. I will call your mother now to let her know you are here and safe, but you can tell her about your face tomorrow," Momma said with concern.

"Okay. I will," said Angel.

Step 87 took me from the living room sofa to the bathroom in the hall close to my room. The blood on Angel's cheek was dripping, so she walked with a napkin she found in her skirt pocket, and used it to catch the constant ooze of blood that came from her cheek. I was afraid it was going to leave a mark. Everyone was always a slight blur to me, but when you're beautiful, you're beautiful, and even I could see that. Angel was gorgeous. She had caramel - cumin complexion, dimples in both cheeks, dark brown eyes with arched eyebrows, and the longest eyelashes humanly possible. If they had been any longer, they would have been on an animal. She was slim but curvy, quite the conversation piece whenever she walked past a group of boys.

As soon as Angel turned on the bathroom light, her cheek was the first thing she saw in the mirror.

"OH NO! I look hideous. Who's going to want to take pictures of me now?" Angel yelled between cries and sniffs. I held her as close and as tightly as I could.

"It's going to be okay, Angel. Trust me. Don't cry. Your tears are going to make it burn more," I warned. Of course, she didn't listen to me; she was too upset. Her cries eventually woke the whole house. Bailey stumbled to the bathroom door with his blue blanket in his hands. He had been carrying that thing everywhere since he could walk. My Momma would always say, "He isn't hurting anyone, so let him carry it." Sometimes Momma forgot to wash it, and it would stink. One of Bailey's big brown eyes was slightly shut, and he looked like he was rubbing the other, or maybe it was his nose. Benny didn't care enough to come and see what was going on. That was typical of him. I knew he was awake. I could feel it. That's how well I knew my brothers.

"What's wrong, Angel?" Bailey said.

"Nothing. Go away, Bailey," she said. She was about to close the door, but Momma and Daddy showed up at the door and intercepted it.

"Angel, don't cry, baby. Let me look at this," Momma said. She examined the cut closely. She told my Daddy to get the first aid kit. "Lean over under the light a little more, baby, so I can see it better," Momma suggested. Angel complied. "This is pretty deep, Angel. You'll need a stitch or two, but it's on the part of your face that will heal well. Is that what you're worried about, baby?" Momma asked.

We all knew that over the last three years Angel had been doing a little print modeling and hoping to make it big. She had been featured in store catalogs for Lord and Taylor, Benetton, and Woodward &Lothrop. Her face seemed to be a big part of her future. We used to always talk about how we were going to be the writer-model duo. I wanted to be the next Terri McMillan, and she wanted to be the next Beverly Johnson. My Daddy showed up with the first aid kit, handed it to my mother, and went back to bed. He took Bailey and escorted him back to bed as well.

"You really think it will heal well, Ms. Pranita?" Angel inquired optimistically.

"I'm 90% sure," Momma said. Momma cleaned her cheek with warm water and a clean gauze. She then placed a little first aid ointment on the cotton part of the band-aid and placed it directly on the open cut. "This should hold for a couple of hours while you sleep, Angel. When you get up, more than likely early afternoon, since it's now 4 AM, Carol and Winston will take you to D.C. General, and in about a month, you'll be as good as new." Momma kissed Angel on the forehead. "Goodnight, girls." Momma left us in the bathroom and went to bed.

"I look ugly, don't I," asked Angel.

"That's impossible," I said. "I can even see how beautiful you are. No one can take that from you." She smiled. I didn't think I was going to see that smile this morning. We walked with Angel's head leaning on my left shoulder. I patted her shoulder reassuringly as we entered my room after step 30. Angel walked over to my full-size bed and reached down to grasp the handle to the bed that was attached to a track that slid back and forth. Momma and Daddy purchased this bed when they realized I had made a friend. A real friend who liked me for me. Angel loosened me up. I stopped talking about serious issues all the time, and eventually I learned to have fun.

We finally settled down to go to sleep. I used my Clap-On device to turn off the lights. "Hey, I wanted to do that," whispered Angel.

"Beat ya to it," I whispered, chuckling sleepily.

CHAPTER TWENTY

"Learning How to Forgive Part II"

"Mistakes are always forgivable if one has the courage to admit them."

Bruce Lee

"OUH!" Angel started moaning loudly. I was still half asleep, but I sat up in bed, reached for my glasses, and saw Angel moaning with her head still on her pillow. "Get Ms. Pranita quick," Angel demanded.

"Okay," I stated, concerned, nervous, and fearful. I sprang out of bed as quickly as I could.

"Ouch! Damn it, Hope!" Angel retorted loudly.

"Oops! My bad," I said. I accidentally stepped on Angel's wrist while trying to get to the door. I wasn't used to the other bed being out. Angel and I hadn't had a sleepover in a year, at least. After step 18, I finally made it to the doorknob. I opened the door hurriedly. "MOMMA, COME QUICK!" I yelled. Momma and Daddy were luckily still in their room when I called, so Momma got to Angel quickly. She walked in with big sponge rollers crowding her head, and still in her satin pajamas.

"Yes, what is it?" Momma inquired.

"Is everything okay, Angel Face?" Miss Carol asked. Miss Carol and Mr. Winston followed Momma into my room. Miss Carol leaned down to talk to Angel.

"Ma, I can't lift my face. It's stuck to the pillow. Every time I try to lift my face, it feels like my skin is being pulled from my cheekbone," Angel said in a whining voice. Miss Carol got down on her knees to get a closer look.

"Did you want a little privacy, Carol and Winston?" My mother asked.

By this time, Angel had the whole Nielson family as her audience. Bailey and Benny were peeking from behind Daddy. They were wearing matching *Hey Arnold* pajamas. I thought by nine years old they would've grown out of cartoon pajamas. I wasn't surprised that they were matching, though, because Bailey and Benny wore everything alike and did everything together. They also had a crush on Angel ever since they started talking, but Bailey was in love; his sad facial expression was understandable. Benny, on the other hand, was a clown statue. He was standing still, barely breathing, with a painted half smile, half smirk on his face. That was such a Benjamin thing to do. My Daddy and I were afraid for Angel. We didn't know what it would look like once Miss Carol detached her face from the pillowcase. I was still half asleep. The night before was a long one.

Miss Carol looked up at the growing audience and said, "Yes, a little privacy would be great." Momma made us all leave. About five minutes later, Angel, Miss Carol, and Mr. Winston entered the kitchen. Angel still had my pillowcase attached to her face. Bailey felt so sorry for Angel. He gave her a cup of orange juice. She drank a little of it and gave him a sweet smile while holding the pillowcase up against her face. It was a little blurry from where I was standing, but I could see the pain hidden behind that smile.

"Thanks for everything, Ms. Pranita," Angel said.

"No problem at all, baby. Don't even mention it. You know you're like a daughter to me. How are you feeling? Are you on the way to D.C. General?" Momma asked.

"Yes, Ma'am," Angel said.

"Thanks so much, Pranita and Pearson. Winston and I are going to see what's going on with this cut. It looks like it scabbed overnight, and the blood and scab may have oozed, dried, and stuck to the pillowcase. Winston and I managed to get the pillow out of the case. It has a little blood on it." Miss Carol was holding the pillow under her arm and her purse under her other arm. "I'm going to take this home and wash it."

"Carol, don't you dare. Don't worry about that silly pillowcase. Concentrate on your baby right now. We got plenty of pillowcases around here. We won't miss that one. Give me that thing, Carol," Momma demanded while pulling the pillow from under Miss Carol's arm.

"That's kind of you, Pranita. Okay, here you go," Miss Carol handed Momma the pillow while Mr. Winston walked Angel outside to the car. Step 55 took me outside to the front porch. Angel was walking slowly, holding her father's arm.

"Wait, I'm coming with you," I yelled.

"You don't have to Hope. I'll be okay. Maybe, I'm not meant to be Beverly Johnson. It's okay," stated Angel.

"I know you'll be okay, and you're going to be better than Beverly Johnson. I'm your best friend, and I'm not letting you go through this alone," I said. Momma came running outside to see what I was doing. I told her I was going with Angel, and she said it was okay. Miss Carol finally made it outside into the car.

As soon as the door closed, Mr. Winston sped off so fast I could barely put my seatbelt on. He turned corners swiftly, yanking my neck and almost making me car sick.

"Slow down, Winston. You don't want to kill the girl before she gets to the hospital," said Miss Carol. Mr. Winston pulled directly in front of the entrance of the emergency room. Miss Carol got out and went to get a wheelchair for Angel. I got out, waiting for Angel to get out of the car. She stood up slowly while moaning and groaning and holding the pillowcase to her face.

I led Angel into the entrance of the hospital. I was guiding her for a change! I was ashamed to admit that it felt kind of nice to be on the other end for once. I found her a seat. The chairs were hard and wobbly but colorful. They were shades of yellow and orange like the walls. D.C. General was an old hospital. It had been there for many years. My mother's uncles and aunts were born at D.C. General. Once I made sure that Angel was okay, I walked to where Miss Carol was standing to see what was going on with the check-in. The lady at the information desk was a stunning shade of mocha and she was sassy. Miss Carol was amazingly patient with her even though mocha-sassy wasn't patient with Miss Carol.

"Ma'am, you gave me the wrong insurance card," she said. I thought you said her name was Angel?"

"It is Angel. Just give me a moment. I have more than one child. It's been a long morning," Miss Carol retorted. Miss Carol finally got fed up with her sassiness and put her in check. "Young lady, it is nice to see you earning an honest living. I admire you for doing something positive. However, there is nothing positive about how you are treating me, a patient's mother who is very worried about her child," Miss Carol stated in a motherly tone.

"Whatever, lady. I don't need your admiration, just your insurance card," said mocha-sassy.

"Young lady, give me a moment, and you will receive what you are requesting as well as a complaint to your manager," Miss Carol retorted.

I was so happy. mocha-sassy took a deep breath and rolled her eyes as Miss Carol rumbled through her purse to look for Angel's insurance card. Mr. Winston finally walked in after finding a parking space and joined us at the information desk.

"Hey honey, is everything okay? Where's Angel?" He inquired while looking a little puzzled about mocha-sassy's facial expression.

"She's sitting in the waiting room, and I'm just trying to find the right insurance card. I have been looking for it for three minutes now, and everything is a mess in my purse. Give me a second, Winston. Why don't you go over where Angel is, babe. You can go too, Hope. I'll be okay up here."

"Are you sure?" I asked.

"Hope If you want to stay, you can," she said in a short tone.

All of a sudden, I smelled a strong aroma. It was a familiar aroma. It smelled like Lagerfeld. My eyes widened. My chest tightened. The smell became stronger and stronger, so I turned around to confirm my suspicion. I didn't know whether to cry, jump for joy, or smack him. My complex emotions ate at me like a lion eating meat. He walked towards me once my smile permitted him to do so. After that, he walked hurriedly in my direction. I wanted to meet him halfway, but he didn't deserve the effort. When he finally reached me, I was flabbergasted. He lifted me off the shiny floor and hugged me tightly.

He whispered in my ear, "I'm so sorry. Please forgive me. I'm lost without you." I looked at his blur of a face. A tear ran down my cheek as I wiped the tears from his cheeks. We entered into a short but passionate kiss and embrace. He planted me back on the floor.

"Okay, I forgive you but don't ever lie to me again," I said. He kissed me again.

"Never again," he said.

"How did you know I was here," I asked.

"Marshall was worried about Angel all night, so finally he asked if I could bring him to her house. We went to her house, and no one was there, so we went to your house. Your little brother Bailey told us that you guys went to D.C. General. Bailey gave Marshall a mean look. What's that about?"

I laughed.

"I'll fill you in on that at another time."

"Marshall is sitting with Angel now, and I immediately went to look for you. Promise me you will never break up with me again," he requested.

"Promise me you will do everything perfectly all the time," I said. Nehemiah chuckled while embracing me.

He whispered to himself, saying," Thank you, God."

CHAPTER TWENTY-ONE
"Beyond Limits"

"Once we accept our limits, we go beyond them."
Albert Einstein

Neha got to my house early the next morning. He rang the doorbell. My Momma opened the door and called for me to come downstairs. Nehemiah was not allowed in my room, so I had to come downstairs, and we talked in the living room as usual. Daddy sat in the dining room. When Nehemiah was around, Daddy was always close by. Neha and I sat on the living room sofa. He kissed me on the cheek and said hello. I was touching my hair and blinking trying to get the crust out of my eyes. I didn't get a chance to do anything to make myself presentable before he got there besides throwing on a hoodie and a pair of shorts. I didn't even know he was coming. He moved my hand as I was trying to make my hair presentable.

He said, "Stop, you look perfect. I want to take you somewhere today."

"Oh yeah, where?" I asked, getting excited.

"It's an adventure. You'll see when you get there."

"Sounds like fun. Okay, let me go get dressed."

"I'll stay here," said Neha.

"You bet your butt you're staying in there," said Daddy from the dining room. Neha laughed, and so did I.

"Go ahead and get dressed, and wear pants and sneakers."

"Oh boy sounds adventurous," I said excitingly. I made my way back to my room as Neha sat patiently on the living room sofa. We had been together for four months, minus the one-day breakup. He knew I was going to be getting ready for a while. I heard him shuffling around the magazines on the coffee table, looking for the remote to the TV. He finally found it and turned it on. My brothers were watching Cartoon Network, so he started watching cartoons. I chuckled to myself and continued to my bedroom.

The ride from D.C. to the adventure was smooth and calming. "Neha, what's up? Where are you taking me? Oh boy! this is where you take me to get even," I inquired jokingly.

"You'll see. Just pump your breaks. We're almost there," said Neha.

"You pump your breaks, Heavy D." I laughed.

Nehemiah leaned toward me and stated in a serious tone, "If you're going to call me anybody, call me Big Daddy Kane. He's the one with the better backup dancers."

"Okay, you got a point. Scoob and Scrap are like that," I said a little defeated.

The pavement changed as we went from the street to the 14th Street Bridge, and then to Interstate 395. It looked as if we were on our way to Virginia, but I wasn't sure if that would be our destination. He continued as I took in the smells of the Potomac River. I was still sleepy, so I leaned back and listened to the birds while feeling the soft breeze from the car window. The pavement changed again, and the motion of the car was different. I sat up and noticed that we were now on the Memorial Parkway, surrounded by Greenery and wind. I was still a bit sleepy because Neha woke me up so early. I decided to lay my head back on the headrest and slept a little until we got to our destination. When I awakened, we were at a park.

"Where are we?" I asked.

"We're at Turner Falls," said Nehemiah.

"What? You are crazy for bringing me here, Neha."

"We're going hiking on Cow's Hoof," he said.

"Hello, legally blind girl here," I said.

"Hey, you can do anything anybody else can do. You got this. Come on. You're going to exercise with me today. I got everything we need in these backpacks. You're going to be fine. I got you."

I stared at Neha's silhouette with confusion and fear as he handed me my backpack, and before I knew it, I was on the trail. As I walked, I broke already crumbled pieces of gravel. The world all of a sudden felt larger than usual. I was surrounded by tall trees with the distant sound of water rushing over a steep cliff. As we walked, an echoing bird call startled me. I squeezed Neha's hand.

"Hey, I gotcha. It was just a few birds," he said. We continued walking down the trail. Everything felt still except moving. The trees spoke to each other as they greeted everything in sight including us. Everything was allowed to invade our space. I closed my eyes as we got closer to the light peeking into the trail. As I closed my eyes, I allowed the forest to tickle my senses with sounds, smells, and feelings.

I felt free! I unclasped Nehemiah's hand, stopped to face the sun, and stretched out my arms to take in all nature had to offer. The wind and sun took turns welcoming me. I allowed them. Nehemiah stood beside me. He did nothing. I assumed he was watching me until I heard his voice from a distance.

"Moon, c'mon girl! Talking to nature," he yelled. I started walking forward, allowing the pieces of ground to collapse under me with every tentative step. Suddenly the trail's pattern started to shift upward. As the terrain changed, I lost my balance, and the sun started to impair my vision. I took one more step and fell to my knees.

"Ouch!" I said. I banged my knee on a large, sharp-edged rock. "Nehemiah!" I called.

"I'm here, Hope. I'm here. Are you okay?"

"No! I'm not okay." I felt blood dripping down my leg as pain pulsated through my knee. "Take me home, Nehemiah. What are you doing? Why am I here?"

"Because I believe in you more than you do," he replied.

I stayed on my knees, gravel piercing my kneecaps like hundreds of little knives. Nehemiah said nothing. I said nothing.

Everything was so still like it was 4AM on the highway. I could hear random hawks cooing in the distance; swaying their wings with liberty. Suddenly Nehemiah's words, my strength, and my need to prove myself lifted me. I rose to my feet and looked up at Neha, who was smiling at me. He was such an old man sometimes. I allowed a smile to overshadow the lightly streaming tears from my strongest eye. As I looked in his direction, my smile gave him permission to embrace me. He hugged me a little tighter than usual, and I felt his chest take a huge sigh of relief.

"Okay, let me go, turkey! I got this!" we unclasped our entangled arms. Neha started laughing.

"Oh, check you out, Heavy D!" He said. I chuckled.

"Are we going to climb this thing or what, man? Let's do this," I said.

Nehemiah took my hand. The path to Cows Hoof continued upward. The scrape on my bottom leg still stung, but I ignored it. Big rocks stuck out of the hill like steps, so we climbed them. Neha had to let go of my hand as the heel got steeper. He needed to keep himself secure. I continued to climb. I smelled the dirt and grass; that's how tightly I hugged the hill. I climbed and climbed and climbed. My fingertips started to burn a little, so I decided to take a break. Once I got to a steady place on the hill, I realized we should have worn gloves. I guessed that was the reason teenagers still lived with their parents. We obviously needed more guidance than we thought.

I continued to climb, reaching higher and higher with every reach and step. The sun became brighter, and climbing became harder. The steps became steeper and steeper the higher I climbed, and so did my bravery. I continued now with much more confidence with every reach and climb. I didn't give up. I reached and climbed. I reached and climbed. I reached and climbed. Just like anywhere else, I traveled. As soon as I established a routine, I was good. It suddenly felt warmer and brighter. My fingernails were filled with mud. That was an uncomfortable feeling. I could still feel Nehemiah nearby. I looked up to see where he was and stepped on a loose rock.

My hands suddenly went flat as I slid a few inches down. Ouch! Ouch! Scud! I caught myself. Debris and mud fell a long distance beneath me. I was afraid to look down. Not because I couldn't see how far but because I was afraid I would lose my balance again. I decided not to panic, although I did swallow a few crumbs of dirt and took a few deep breaths. I leaned against the grass and gravel for a few minutes to collect myself. Nehemiah had already made it to the top.

"You okay, Heavy D? You can do it. Keep climbing, Moon. You got this," he yelled. His voice motivated me. I started stepping on one rock at a time and grabbing large pieces of gravel. I continued my rhythm; reach and climb. reach and climb, reach and climb. It became a rhythm, step grab, step grab, step grab until finally, one last grunt, grab step, and I made it. Neha grabbed my hand to lift me onto the top of the hill. I did it! I wished he could read my mind, but I'm sure the huge grin of excitement on my face was enough to communicate my triumph. "You did it!" He said. He started singing Heavy D lyrics in my ear. *Now that we found love what are we gonna do with it?* With all the excitement, Nehemiah picked me up to celebrate. I was caught off-guard so much that I leaned too much of my weight on him. Neha lost his balance on the loose gravel. As he leaned to catch himself, I slipped out of his arms and went face-first into the brown mixture of dirt and rock. I tried to grab and reach, but it was too late. I screamed. I was falling! I lost control of all of my limbs.

"Oh God, oh God!" I screamed. I heard Nehemiah's yells and groans from a distance. I hit one last rock. Gunk! I landed. "Oh, God! Somebody help! Oh, God!" I cried.

CHAPTER TWENTY-TWO

"Only the Strong Survive"

"The weak can never forgive. Forgiveness is the attribute of the strong."

Mahatma Gandhi

My surroundings were blurrier than usual. I couldn't see Nehemiah's usual brown silhouette. Instead, he was a hazy black. My ears still worked fine. For a while, his voice rang strong, but as the constant screams of my name grew faint, everything was still, even the birds that called and cooed grew faint. I wanted to pass out, but my adrenaline wouldn't let me. I tried to move my legs and arms, but the sharp pain and spreading numbness overpowered me. I lifted myself a little with a grunt, but it was no use. I laid on the ground helpless, afraid, and wondering what the hell was taking Nehemiah so long to find me.

I wasn't paralyzed, thank God, because I felt a nasty little critter crawling on my legs. I crouched down to flick it off. Boy, did that hurt! I tried again without success to lift myself onto my feet. The mountain itself started to move as I opened my eyes. I kept my head up, about three inches from the ground, for about 30 seconds, and then everything went dark! When I opened my eyes again, a familiar face stared down at me. I could faintly make out the hair. The figment was so close. It got even closer.

"Are you okay?" The familiar voice asked.

"I'll be okay. Can you help me sit up?" I said.

"I think I've watched enough Doogie Howser to know I shouldn't move you," she chuckled. What happened? Did you fall?"

"No dah," I whispered under my breath. "Yes, I fell."

"Are you here alone?" She asked, even though I was sure she already knew the answer.

"I'm here with…" Before I could fully answer, Nehemiah arrived with the paramedics. I could hear the sound of a helicopter a short distance away.

"Oh God, are you okay, Moon? I was so worried. It was hell getting down that ravine in a hurry, and then I had to run back to the car to use the phone and call for help. I'm so sorry it took me so long to get to you." Nehemiah finished his dissertation of excuses and then tried to embrace me.

"Don't move her," demanded the paramedic." We don't know the extent of her injuries." Nehemiah stooped down and kissed me on the cheek.

Figment was still there standing and watching the paramedics prepare me for the stretcher. Neha couldn't believe his eyes. It was Yevette. I was surprised she didn't pick up a rock and finish me off!

"What are you doing here, Yvette? Are you following me?" Neha inquired with obvious irritation in his voice.

"No, I come here sometimes to clear my head, but I'm not going to lie; I did follow you two to the trail when I saw ya'll enter the park. I was just curious, Neha. I didn't mean you and Hope any harm," she said. She walked over to the stretcher. Please tell Neha I tried to help you. I'm so sorry you fell. I hope you be okay." She touched my hand with endearment.

"Thanks for your help, Yvette." I cupped my hand over hers as I spoke. Nehemiah gave Yvette the keys to his car, so she could call my parents from his car phone.

The helicopter ride was more peaceful than I thought. I could hear the rhythmic sounds of voices jumping out of the walkie-talkies and radio receivers. Neha held my hand while the paramedic adjusted my IV bag.

"You're going to be okay, Moon. I know it. I can't imagine life without you," he said. I smiled, but suddenly my fingertips started to tingle and my lips became very numb. I faintly heard, "Her vitals are not good. I'm losing her." I felt pressure on my chest as Neha screamed, "NO!!!!"

CHAPTER TWENTY-THREE

"Prayers for a Miracle"

"For man, as for flower and beast and bird, the supreme triumph is to be most vividly, most perfectly alive".

D. H. Lawrence

I woke up once again in a hospital bed. This time it was much different. My eyes were open, and everything around me was clear! I did not understand. My mother's skin wasn't its usual grayish tan, but the back of her neck was perfectly tan and clear. I could even see the crease in the back of her neck. The doctor's lab coat wasn't its usual beige blur. It was perfectly white or perfectly beige. I've never seen clear enough to know the difference. I overheard them talking. My hearing wasn't as sharp as usual, but I could still hear their conversation.

"Doctor, what are the odds of her sight remaining post-surgery?" Momma inquired.

"As I explained to you before, the surgery, Mrs. Neilson, is strictly experimental. However, in 70% of the cases, the patients have fully regained their sight and maintained it for at least ten years, and as far as I know, 50% of them surpassed that ten year mark and are still living without further impairment."

"Well, either way, my girl will be just fine!" Momma walked over to my bedside. "She's awake! Praise God!" Momma got on her knees, stretched her arms out, and proceeded to do what some Christians call, catching the Holy Spirit! Yup, right in the hospital room in front of the doctor, and nurses. "Hallelujah, hallelujah, praise God!" Tears ran down her cheeks as she repeated this over and over again.

Daddy, Angel, and Nehemiah must have heard her from the hall because they came storming in. Daddy rushed over to Momma and knelt down beside her. I could hear him say softly, "Pranita, baby calm down. I agree, He is powerful, graceful, and merciful, and I thank Him too, but you are disturbing the other ill patients in this wing." Momma calmed down, but she stayed on her knees and started a silent prayer.

We were a very spiritual family. Every room had an open Bible lying on a desk or nightstand. We had the Bible in Braille. Bailey, Benny, and I were required to read a verse a night from Genesis to Revelations. I thought to myself, God is so wonderful. I could see everyone in the room at that moment so clearly. It was a miracle! I also felt my limbs; however, I did have a pounding headache. Daddy walked over to the bed. He was taller than I thought. I'd been concentrating on trying to see his face and body as a whole for so long, and he just seemed shorter.

"How are you feeling, my girl?" he asked. I squinted for the first time in my life to see clearer, but that was only because I had a splitting headache, not because I was trying to correct blurred vision.

"So, so, Daddy. I have a throbbing headache. You think they can get me some medicine or something for this?"

"I'm sure they can," Daddy said. "I'll check, but they'll probably want to examine you a little first."

The doctor already examined me. He said I looked good! I think Mama made him a little uncomfortable when she was praising the Lord," I stated.

"You've been in a coma for two weeks, baby," Daddy shared. I gasped.

"Yes, God is good all the time," said Momma.

"Two weeks, huh?" I asked.

"Yes, and Nehemiah has done nothing but sit here by your bedside. I don't think he's been to basketball practice, class, or even home. Has he Pearson?" Momma said with admiration.

"He went home a couple of times, and I've seen him do homework, but otherwise, he's been sitting next to you, Moon," Momma said empathetically.

Once Angel and Neha saw Momma worshiping, they figured we could use some family time, so they left the room again.

"He was?" I asked with a sentimental smile. I was always overjoyed about anything to do with Neha, but this made me so overjoyed. I couldn't control my smiles and what was going on with my heart.

"Yes, he did. He got better after a couple of days at controlling his crying during the first week. You could only hear his muffled murmurs! He's a fine, dedicated, and sensitive man. Sounds like a keeper to me," Momma said with her hands on her hips and her lips primped with a sassy expression.

"I don't know about all that, but I was impressed with his dedication, though," Daddy said, stroking my dry coils. "How are you feeling? How's your sight? You had some hemorrhaging in your head, so they had to perform emergency surgery."

I gasped! "Oh no! Are you serious, Daddy?" I was in shock. Momma chimed in.

"Yes, they did. The neurosurgeon had some background on your eye disease and told your Daddy and me about a new experimental treatment. The odds of seeing clear and keeping your sight without impairment are fairly good, so how's your sight right now?" She asked.

"Fairly good. What are the stats?" I said with concern.

"70% of the patients who received the treatment saw clearly for ten years, and 50% kept their sight without further impairment. I'm going to ask you one more time. Alexandria Hope Nielson, how is your sight?" Momma's nostrils got bigger than usual. I guess this coma of mine had taken its toll on her. I let out a deep, annoyed sigh and answered.

"My sight is amazing right now, Momma. I see every blondish-brown hair on your head. I see the pointy Indian nose that me, Benny, and Bailey share with you. I see the footboard at the end of this hospital bed. I see the bright fluorescent lights and the long bulbs under the white shades that cover them! I see my handsome father, who carries his blue-black African ancestry over every inch of him." I started to cry. It felt so refreshing and new! "I can see, Momma!" I sat up in my bed abruptly. Ouch, too soon." Damn, I have a splitting headache," I said.

"Be careful, Moon, and watch your mouth. You've been in a coma for two weeks! You're blessed to have only that; a concussion and a sprained ankle. I'd say you're doing quite well. Let me get the nurse," said Daddy.

"Okay, thanks, Momma." The nurse came in with a miniature white cup containing two orange pills. The word ibuprofen was printed in small letters on each of them. I couldn't believe I could read that! I used the water on my rollaway table that swung over my bed to take the pills as fast as I could. My head was still throbbing, but I found comfort in knowing that the medicine would eventually kick in. I remained sitting up because I enjoyed seeing clearly so much; the feeling was all that and two bags of chips! It was a feeling I never wanted to end! After about 15 minutes, the ibuprofen kicked in, and just in time, because I would have never been able to handle what came next with a throbbing headache.

"We're going down to the cafeteria before it closes. Do you want anything, Moon? Your doctor didn't put you on any diet restrictions," Momma said.

"No, Momma, I'm okay. Thanks for asking, I replied.

"Okay, Daddy's Baby, we'll be right back. Take it easy; the nurse's button is right beside you, but you've probably seen it already," Daddy chuckled after that last remark and walked out the door.

"Hi," a voice said to my parents as they exited.

"How are you doing?" Momma uttered as she began to exit the door. "Hope, you have a visitor, baby," said Momma.

CHAPTER TWENTY-FOUR

"The Power of Forgiveness"

"Darkness cannot drive out darkness; only light can do that. Hate cannot drive out hate; only love can do that."

Martin Luther King, Jr.

Yvette looked so nervous, and now I literally saw her with fresh eyes. She was not too bad! She had her hair in long braids that hit her waist. She was really light-skinned; she looked almost White, but her hair wasn't as fine. It was frizzy and thick around the edges, but if you weren't looking closely, you would think she was white. When she wasn't being mean and envious, you could hear her melodious Jamaican accent. It was beautiful! I guess that's why she and Nehemiah connected. I think they were both from Kingston, Jamaica; although, Nehemiah lost his accent completely. It was cute and funny the way he said certain words sometimes. She walked slowly and carefully approaching my hospital bed.

"Hi," she said.

"How are you doing?" I said.

"I came a couple of times when you were in a coma. Don't worry, I didn't try to rekindle anything with Nehemiah. He made it very clear that you are the one he wants to be with.

When I came the first time, I came to see if you were all right. I heard you fell into a coma during the helicopter ride. I saw you fall down the hill, Hope." Her face drooped with sadness. "I'm not going to lie; I was glad at first. I mean I didn't want you to die or nothing. I'm really glad you are okay, let's be clear. I was just so jealous of you and Nehemiaha's relationship, but I see the way he looks at you. It is real and special. I wanted that so much for him and I, but I have accepted it now, and I wish you two the best!" She got a little hoarse because she was getting a little choked up.

"I appreciate you coming, Yvette. It's nice of you, and thanks for helping me when I was lying helpless on the ground out there," I said with both hands laying on my heart.

"No problem, I was really scared for you. I thought you were dead! I hated you, Hope, but I never wanted you to die." She paused, and we looked into each other's eyes with genuine respect for each other.

"Well, take care of yourself. I heard you got your sight back. That's good. Now you can see how much cuter I am than you." She smiled jokingly. "Hope to see you around campus soon. Ha Ha, no pun intended," she chuckled.

"That would be cool," I said.

She tiptoed out of the room. I guess she thought all sick people sleep all the time. Her braids swung from side to side as she began to stroll out. She took about seven steps and stopped. Angel walked in with Neha. Angel couldn't believe her eyes. She took a really long pause while looking Yvette up and down.

Suddenly she started to aggressively move toward her. Neha grabbed Angel's arms. My feet were about to swing out of the sheets to stop her, but Neha had it under control.

"Angel, let it go," Neha demanded. Yvette became a whole different person. Her chest leaned forward towards Angel with her fists balled up. She was ready for battle, but Neha stood in the middle between both of them. Yvette brushed Neha's hand from her shoulder. "I'm alright, Nehemiah," she uttered calmly. Yvette was a chameleon. She took on a whole new form instantly. She grabbed the doorknob and started to leave after giving me one last wave goodbye.

"Look, Angel, why don't you learn some respect and manners and stay out of my face. Angel moved closer to Yvette aggressively again, but Nehemiah caught her wrist just in time.

"I have manners! What are you even doing here? Go back to whatever hole you crawled out of," Angel retorted.

"I came to see Hope. Say all the mean things you want, Angel. That's why Marshall only talks to you when he has nothing else to do. Why I'm here is none of your business." Yvette struck an emotional nerve. I could tell that Angel was hurt. "Yvette, please leave," Neha demanded while trying to control Angel's very physical hostility.

"Gladly," she retorted. Yvette opened the door to leave. She turned abruptly, allowing her braids to paint the air like a paintbrush moving swiftly on a canvas. Angel, in restraint, snarled at what used to be where Yvette was standing. and as soon as the door closed, two nurses barged in. Only one of them spoke to us. I assumed the other one came for crowd control.

"Is everything okay here?" Asked the tallest one of the two.

"Yes, everything is fine. We apologize for the disturbance," I answered. The tallest one was my nurse.

"Okay, well, not only should you be getting your rest, but there is a hospital full of people who need their rest as well, so the yelling has to stop," said the tallest one. We all wore expressions of embarrassment as we looked on like scolded siblings who broke an important house rule.

"We understand, Ma'am. It won't happen again," Neha somberly stated.

"Thank you, young man, I appreciate that. While I'm here, I'm going to check your vitals, Alexandra. Is this a good time?"

"Sure, no problem," I uttered, raising myself up and shifting my sheets and blankets. Nehemiah sat down to finish the soda he left on the floor beside the orange vinyl chair, and Angel sat on the foot of my bead. The tall nurse wrapped a blue velcro device around my skinny biceps, something I had never really noticed before about me. I heard a subtle click, and my arm was instantly on fire, and then it started to cool. The nurse snatched open the device and removed it from my bicep. She looked over my body.

"You look good, Alexandra. Please get some rest. I recommend that your visitors leave soon."

"Yes, ma'am," I said. I looked directly at Angel as she moved closer to me from the foot of the bed. Angel looked the same to me, just clearer. The scar was almost completely healed. You could barely see it on her cheek. It had been two weeks since the party. The day Yvette scared her face. I didn't realize that it went back so far. It started right on her cheekbone and ended at her ear. I tried to focus on her eyes instead of the scar, so she wouldn't be uncomfortable.

"Can you actually see me, Hope? I mean, am I a clear image or a shadowy figure with blurred features?" Angel inquired.

"Yes, I can see you clearly. Iman, look out!"

"I don't know about all that. What modeling agency will want to scout me with this hideous scar on my face? Face it, Hope. My dream of being a model is over. Oh, and by the way, I haven't heard from Marshall in a couple of days either," she replied.

Nehemiah interrupted the beginning of his nap to look at Angel, shaking his head in disgust with Marshall. "Classic Marshall, always running away when life gets difficult," stated Neha. I reached out to hold Angel's hand.

"Don't give up on him. It's only been a couple of days. Maybe he just doesn't know how to deal with this type of situation. It could be too much for him with his girlfriend getting hurt and," Angel interrupted me.

"Wait! Wait! I didn't say anything about being his girlfriend. Don't get ahead of yourself. It's only been two weeks. And for disappearing, he'll be lucky if we're still on speaking terms," declared Angel.

"Well, I was in a coma, you got into a brawl at his house, and I'm sure Neha has been leaning on him through all of this. That's a lot, Angel."

"Why do you always act like an old lady? He was fine after the party. He came to the hospital to see me. Ain't nothing wrong with Marshall. He's just an ass-tronaut." I blurted hysterically into laughter.

"I get it. Ass-tro-naut." We laughed and laughed. Angel lost her balance and held on to the bar of the hospital bed. We looked at Nehemiah. He was still sound asleep on the orange vinyl recliner. His brown curly locks were pointed in sporadic directions as his neck laid comfortably on the back of the chair. We were still and quiet for about 20 seconds listening to his soft song of breathing and snoring. I looked at Angel and exploded into laughter again.

"He can be an Ass-stronaut too, sometimes!" Angel immediately mimicked my same humorous emotion. We laughed and laughed until we finally settled down.

"Move over, Moon," she said. I slid my pillow and blankets to one side to make room for her. Her right arm clasped my available arm, and we allowed our heads to meet and hold each other up like floats. That's what we were for each other. Angel and I were always keeping ourselves from sinking.

"I missed you, Moon. That was the longest two weeks of my life. I thought I lost my best friend." Angel tightened our clasp. I was trying to hold back the tears, but it was no use. Once I felt her tears on my cheek, mine began to roll. So we cried, and sobbed. We paused and looked over at Neha. He was still sound asleep. He was completely unbothered, but his mouth was open this time, allowing his breathing and snoring to sang a duet. Angel and I unclasped our arms, leaned over, listening to the duet, and exploded into laughter again. We looked at the corpse again and laughed even harder, trying to muffle our symphony of happy noise. It didn't work. Before we knew it, Nehemiah's eyes opened. We gasped as if we were caught doing something wrong. Our eyes locked on each other. We all paused in awkward silence.

"What?" Neha said.

"Nothing," we said in unison. Angel and I looked at each other again with conspiratorial grins, then threw our heads back on the bed and enjoyed another burst of laughter.

CHAPTER TWENTY-FIVE

"New Paths"

"Amazing Grace, How sweet the sound That saved a wretch like me "

John Newton

Everything had always been a blur or some colors mixed with grayish undertones. Sometimes if the light was right, I got lucky enough to see a somewhat clear image of what was in front of me if it was close enough, and I was wearing my goggles. Today as the nurse rolled me out to my Mom's car, the sun was the brightest it's ever been. My mother, father, Benny, and Bailey had a golden backdrop behind them that made them glow like aliens visiting from another planet. My Momma, Daddy, Benny, and Bailey stared at me strangely, maybe because my pupils looked more focused and normal.

"Well, don't just stand there. Let's go. I'm ready to be out," I said. Bailey left my family's side and walked hurriedly towards me. His short skinny caramel legs looked thicker than usual because of his slouchy socks. Those socks were magical. They could transform all sets of string bean legs into normal-sized calves. Although my little brothers were Irish twins that looked like identical twins, there was still a noticeable difference between him and Benjamin. Bailey had always been slightly smaller, and although they both had beige curly locks that looked like sand scattered all over their heads, Bailey's curls were always bigger and more defined. Bailey came closer to me, still wearing a look of confusion. He examined every crevice of my face as if I were a ghost. "Hi, Baileyboo. How are you?"

"I'm fine, Moon," he uttered, staring at me like I was a sentence in a complex novel that was really hard to comprehend. "Why were you asleep so long? I thought you were going to die," he said while holding out his arms, inviting me to embrace his scrawny little body. I extended my arms to grab him and responded to his question. I squeezed him tighter than the time he found my favorite necklace for me. I had a huge lump in my throat. I couldn't imagine leaving my little brothers.

"I scared you, Baileyboo?" I said while maintaining our embrace.

"Yeah, I thought you weren't coming back. Momma kept going in your room rearranging the pillows on your bed and straightening the stuff on your desk, you know, all the pens and books you won't let me and Benny touch. Benny reads your journal sometimes without you knowing. He went in a couple of times while you were sleeping at the hospital, and I saw him writing in one of your journals instead of reading." He looked up at me, smiling and appreciating my presence. I smiled back.

"Bailey, I'm sorry I scared you," I stated as I hugged him tighter. Before I could utter my next sentence, Benny walked over and interrupted. He ran over towards me like I was one of his opponents at one of his little league football games, except when he reached me, I was knocked off balance, and he wrapped his long sandy arms around me and squeezed instead of trying to tackle me to the ground. His words were slightly muffled because his head was buried under my armpit, but I heard him.

"Me too, Moon. You scared me too." I looked down at Benny and his slightly bigger arms, legs, and smaller curls, and stared at him with tear-filled eyes.

"Even though you're still a donkey head," he said, hugging me again. I pulled both of them close, and we all stood still for 30 seconds, thankful to be reunited.

"Cmon, my babies, I want to hit the road before it gets crowded with rush hour traffic," Momma ordered as she opened the back car door for me. Daddy was already in the driver's seat, and Bailey, Benny, and I looked at Momma and moved immediately at her demand.

"Moon?"

"Yes, Momma?"

"I know you heard what the doctor said. Take it easy and get plenty of rest." Her light brown eyes gave me a warning all on their own.

"Momma, I've been sleeping for two weeks. Don't you think I've had enough rest?" She turned abruptly in my direction as Daddy turned onto Benning Road.

"Watch the sass, Hope. WATCH THE SASS!" She demanded. Momma's voice got drastically sassy and very stern. I proceeded with caution because I knew Momma didn't play. I shut up after that. I didn't want Momma's attitude to reach 1000. I knew my boundaries with Mrs. Pranita Keen Nielson. We continued to drive along, piled in the 92 Honda, and listened to Momma sing along with the radio. She knew every song, word for word. She loved that cool old people's music from the sixties and seventies. I learned to love it too. There were so many amazing artists. I started thinking about Aretha Franklin's songs like "R-E-S-P-E-C_T" and "Natural Woman." I hoped that those two songs were every woman's anthem. Neither one of them came on the radio this time, so Momma sang the James Brown song they played instead. She always had the same posture when she enjoyed a song. Both of her arms were raised up as high as the car roof would allow, and she sang along, "I feel good. Like I knew that I would...." She clapped and sang, and yelled, and laughed. Bailey, Benny, and I looked on as Daddy joined her, and his actions permitted us to join. We all had a family sing-along with James Brown. The song repeated the verse again and again, and so did we, as loud and free as we wanted. In Unison, "I FEEL GOOD... I KNEW THAT I WOULD. I FEEL GOOD... I KNEW THAT I WOULD. SO GOOD! SO GOOD! I GOT YOU!"

The house smiled when I arrived as if it were glad to see me too. It wasn't Marshall or Nehemiah's house, but it was gorgeous and it was my home. I had never noticed the royal blue shutters, the red brick, and all the shiny windows. The door was wack though! Momma painted it yellow. That door didn't match anything. The brick was a dark and clean red, the shutters were royal blue, and the window trim was a shiny white as if it were freshly painted. All of the porch furniture was white wicker with royal blue cushions. So why was the door yellow? Momma mustv'e had a moment! I guess she wanted to make sure I always came to the right house.

Daddy parked right in front of the mailbox dressed in stickers and three multi-colored welcome home balloons. I smiled and leaned towards the front seats of the car. "Thanks, Fam!" I said while taking in the mosaic of landscaped lawns, and neatly configured furniture on various porches. Turquoise, tangerine, red, and yellow cushions were neatly placed on chairs and rockers while exotic plants in big ceramic pots were placed strategically in the sun's path. My mother kept our yard pristine. She never wanted me to trip over anything accidentally, so everything was always neatly kept in its place as I remembered it. Now that I could see, they were not only neatly placed but beautifully coordinated. She decided to tie in the yellow door. The patio set consisted of two white wicker rocking chairs and a wicker loveseat covered with big fluffy, yellow paisley cushions with specks of royal blue. The two columns on the porch that gave it its royal look had two large mustard yellow ceramic pots with Chinese Evergreens planted around them. In addition, a round glass coffee table was placed in front of the wicker loveseat and a yellow ceramic ashtray was neatly placed in the middle for my father's cigar-smoking pleasure. Momma looked at me with eyes the color of ginger and smiled back in my direction.

"I'm glad you like them, Moon. Bailey picked them out," Momma said as she attempted to get out of the parked car. I looked over at Bailey with his perfectly round head and

Momma's eyes and leaned over to give him a huge kiss on his fluffy curls.

"Thanks, Baileyboo," I uttered under my puckered lips. I could feel his smile of satisfaction without even looking at him.

"Race ya," Benny yelled while running up the stairs and looking back at Bailey. As we approached the door, I spied the doorknob and keyhole.

"Wait, Momma," I requested.

"Everything okay, Moon?" Momma inquired.

"You okay, Moon? Daddy questioned.

"I'm fine. I just want to use the key to unlock the door for the first time in my life. Can I do that, Daddy?"

"Of course, you can," Daddy and Momma answered simultaneously. He pushed back all the other keys on his ring. For some reason, Daddy's keys were always heavier and much louder than Momma's. I accepted the pointy silver key from him. The keyhole looked at me in amazement, and I looked back at it like a discovery. I slid the key into its crevices and unlocked the door all by myself. If I were a guy, I would've been "The Man."

CHAPTER TWENTY-SIX

"How precious did that grace appear
The hour I first believed"

Amazing Grace by John Newton

The door opened, and a big "SURPRISE" rang from every crevice of the house. Everyone was there. Marshall, a surprise, Neha, Angel, Ms. Carol, Mr. Winston, Angel's two brothers, Ms. Maverick, Grandma Keen, Grandma Nielson, and a couple of the neighbors I only observed Momma and Daddy wave to from time to time. Our one-level rambler seemed bigger. I guess because I could see Momma's wall-papered living room and her jade-green sectional draped with bodies. I saw people standing along the long hallway stretched to the backdoor past Momma's sewing room. Unfamiliar faces lined up along the hallway near the kitchen, and along the hall near the sewing room doorway, trying to get a glimpse of my reaction. I was honored and shocked at the same time. I hugged as many people as I could, but there were too many people all examining me like I was a new exhibit.

I hugged my two grandmothers tightly. My mother's mother looked just like my mother. Grandma Keen was light-eyed, caramel, and curvy. I walked to the recliner where her curves fit perfectly on the chair as she sat like a queen on her throne. The white curtains behind her hanging on the large bay window looked like a backdrop presenting her as royalty.

"Hello, Grandma Keen," I said as I embraced her.

"Hi, Baby. How are you feeling?" She whispered as she squeezed me with an embrace of concern and relief. "You know you sho' did scare us. You're Momma practically lost her mind. I don't even remember her sleeping. I stayed with her cause your Daddy had to go to work. You know the government don't want to hear of no Black man taking too many days off, Chile, sickness or not," she stated, sipping on her fountain coke and ending it with, an ahhh!

"Yes, I know what you mean, Grandma Keen!" I laughed.

"I have been here at the house for two weeks now. You slipped into that coma in the ambulance, and Pranita called from the hospital in a panic mess. I couldn't even hear what she was saying. She was yelling so loud, so I just hung up the phone and drove on up here." Grandma Keen grabbed my hand and held her lips tucked in together and tightly like she did when she was feeling deep emotion. "I'm just glad you're alright, Baby. Just glad you're alright." I hugged her tightly.

"I'm glad too, GK. I'm glad too." Grandma Nielson walked over like a Mocha satin doll. She didn't always have a lot to say. She was just glad I was still smart and okay. I hugged her tightly too. The love I had for my grandmothers was endless.

CHAPTER TWENTY-SEVEN

"A dream Deferred"

"Through many dangers, toils, and snares
I have already come,
'Tis grace has brought me safe thus far
And grace will lead me home."
Amazing Grace by John Newton

"Momma," I said softly, cuddled beside her. She looked so tired. I was glad everyone went home. It was really nice to see them all, and I appreciated all of the kind words and love, but I could tell Momma was over it after a while and wanted to rest.

"Yes, Moon?"

"I'm sorry," I stated as I wiped the emotion clean from my face.

"What are you sorry for, Baby? You have nothing to be sorry about," she replied while rubbing my back.

"Yes, I do. I shouldn't have gone with Nehemiah on that mountain. I could barely see in front of me. Why did I think I could climb a mountain?"

"So why did you do it?" She inquired with somewhat of a frown on her face but mostly a look of curiosity.

"I'm trying to build my story, Momma. You have so many wonderful adventures that you tell that are so compelling. I hang on to your every word when you share them with me. I'm a writer without a story, Momma. How annoying is that? I have so much to say but nothing to tell." Momma raised up so she could be at eye level with me.

"Moon, I understand that you are trying to find your story, but you don't have to almost kill yourself to do that. Your stories will find you. The more you live and allow yourself to be vulnerable and experience things, the more stories you'll have to tell," she stated softly while gently pinching my chin and moving my face in her direction. "Just keep living, Moon. Just keep living."

"Okay, Momma, I will." I rested my head on Daddy's pillow. He was in the living room. He was probably watching sports and smoking a cigar.

"Momma?"

"Yes, Moon," she answered while yawning and resting her eyes in a sleepy posture, her body was sitting up straight on her pillow and her head was slightly leaning forward.

"I love those stories from long ago, but I wonder why we only speak about the past." She woke up quickly as if my question fueled her.

"Moon, the past is a roadmap to the future. It's your blueprint. Those experiences show you what worked and didn't; what path to continue to follow and which direction we should never take again. The past lays the foundation for who you will become in the future. It helps you explain some of the qualities or actions you see in yourself in the present. We need the past even as early as yesterday. It helps guide our steps today and can be very entertaining." She chuckled as she made that last statement.

"Okay, Momma. Goodnight. Get some rest." I laughed and nodded in profound thought and agreement. I kissed her forehead and left the room. As I exited the door, I heard a faint and sleepish "Goodnight, Moon."

The next morning, I got up bright and early to go jogging with Neha at our favorite park. It seemed like after speaking with Momma last night, I got a burst of energy. Usually, I was out of breath trying to keep up with Nehemiah going around the park. That day he was struggling to keep up with me. I got in front of him and jokingly started jogging backwards. "Who's your mama?" I stated with confidence.

"Oh, you got jokes? I was out late with Marshall last night, so don't get too happy, Ms. Alexandra Hope. It will never happen again," he said with a smirk. He opened his arms and grabbed me playfully, lifting me off the ground a little like he would often do. My feet started dangling as my lips puckered to kiss him, but instead, he allowed me to land softly on the grass as he sprinted past me.

"You cheater," I yelled.

"Don't hate the player. Hate the game," he yelled back from the other end of the park.

"Whatever! You sore loser! Let's go eat. I'm hungry," I yelled back.

"Okay, race you to the car," he said. I realized that his mother's BMW that he borrowed for the day was parked closest to where I was, so I ran for it. With the wind beating me in the face, I sprinted faster than ever. I felt Neha's footsteps coming closer, vibrating the ground like a giant. He must've been moving at incredible speed because before I reached the car, Neha grabbed me from behind, and we fought for the finish line. Somehow, I got strength from somewhere and dragged him behind me to the hood of his mother's car.

"I win," I yelled triumphantly. I raised my hands in the air, put my feet on my tippy-toes, and did the touchdown dance teasingly in Neha's face.

"I let you win, little girl!" He declared. The light from the glistening sunlight must have made me radiant to Neha because he pulled my hand forcefully, moving my whole body in one passionate tug. I ended up enveloped in his arms with my lips squished against his. The kiss was powerful, passionate, and never-ending. I'd never felt the way I was feeling! The temperature within my body was at least 200 degrees. His heavy muscular body pressed the back of my head firmly on the car window. I could feel his muscles bulge on every part of his body. He desperately wanted parts of me that no one had ever touched before. I was a prize. I was nervous. I had never felt that way before. Parts of my body were pulsating like electromagnetic waves.

"Moon?" He whispered while a part of his lips still brushed mine.

"Hmm?" I answered, still pulsating with affection.

"Can we take this somewhere private?" Suddenly all the waves in me paused. I didn't know what to say. Momma talked to me about this many times, but I never dreamed the moment would come, and before I knew it, a "YES" flew out of my mouth, and then we were suddenly somewhere private.

The leather seats were cold on my back. We continued the same rhythmic dance of passion we started outside. He kissed my body as I ran my fingers through his big silky locks until all of him became a part of all of me.

After, he laid his head on my shoulder. I placed my fingers on the exposed part of his face.

"I love you, Moon. Just know that this was special. You are my forever, and I hope you feel the same way," he stated while gently rubbing my arm up and down as if he were applying oil.

"I pictured my first time differently. I thought I would be somewhere a little more appropriate. Not the backseat of your mother's car."

"Did you hear me say I love you, Moon, and this is how you respond?" He retorted.

"I love you too, Nehemiah. Yes, I feel the same way. I'm just glad we are the only ones parked here." Neha started laughing. As we drove away from the park, I looked back at the parking space as if I had left something valuable behind.

CHAPTER TWENTY-EIGHT

"Dreams Possibly Deferred"

"What happens to a dream deferred?

Does it dry up

like a raisin in the sun?

Or fester like a sore—

And then run?"

From Harlem by Langston Hughes

Ringgggggg! Ringgggggg! Angel was ringing the doorbell like a crazy person. Thank God my parents weren't home.

"Are you sure?" She asked emphatically, holding my hands and looking at me as if she was searching for something lost.

"Well, I'm sure I didn't get my period if that's what you're asking."

"What in the world, Hope? Did you even take a pregnancy test?" She asked.

"What? No. I don't know. I thought you had to go to a clinic for that," I said, confused. Angel's eyes rolled up in her head. I could tell she was frustrated with me, but the good news was her scar was completely gone.

"Girl, your face looks beautiful. What did you use?"

"Hope, don't skip the subject. You may be knocked up! The hell with my face right now. There are 'in-home' pregnancy tests that you can use."

"You mean I have to take my blood? I'm not doing that, Angel."

"No dummy. Where have you been?"

"Uh, been kinda blind."

"Oh, that's right. Sorry."

"Well, we can go to the drugstore and pick up a pregnancy test. All you have to do is pee on a stick and wait a few minutes to find out. I'm sorry, Hope, but I have to ask this. Did you use protection that failed you?"

"What's protection?" I inquired, perplexed.

"Oh my God! What are you, 12 or 17?"

"Again, been blind! Blind people don't watch TV. I also never thought I would ever have a boyfriend, and obviously, my mother thought so, too, because all she ever told me was not to do it. She shared nothing about how to protect myself from this."

"Well, I blame Ms. Pranita because I can't keep Ms. Carol from talking about the risks of having sex, sexually transmitted diseases, getting pregnant and having to take care of a baby I'm not ready for."

"Wait! Shoot! Could I catch a disease from doing this? Oh, my God! Oh, my God! Oh, my God!" I repeatedly stated as I paced up and down my living room floor.

"Calm down. Calm down. Yes, all of that is possible. The good news is that the athletes have to undergo an intensive health screening once every few months, so you may be able to rule out a disease." Stated Angel confidently.

"That makes me feel a little bit better," I replied.

"I would see your doctor to make sure. Let's go to the drugstore and rule out pregnancy, and buy you some protection. Who has time for babies or diseases? C'mon! What is wrong with Ms. Pranita not talking to you about this?" Angel stated in disgust and disappointment.

"Forgive my mom, Angel. Having a blind child is a lot of work," I sighed. The drugstore was within walking distance. Angel and I didn't have our licenses yet. We ran to the drugstore at the strip mall behind our community as fast as we could.

The choice of pregnancy tests were overwhelming. I didn't know what to buy. All of them had a picture of a white or yellow stick attached to a part that looked wider than the top of an hourglass. When I read the box of each one, the directions were similar. Wet the tip of the stick with pee and wait for a certain symbol that either stood for positive or negative. I bought two of them to be sure.

When I got home, my parents' car was parked in the driveway. Angel thought it was a good idea to do the test at her house. Not to mention, she had her own bathroom in her room. Mr. Winston installed it for her when she turned 13. We walked into her house wearing expressions of something to hide, but her parents didn't ask any questions. All we got was a hello from Ms. Carol and a nod from Mr. Winston. We hurried to Angel's room and tore open both boxes. I started reading the directions again.

"Damn it, Hope, you read it at the store," she exclaimed, frustrated and holding both unused tests in her hand. I grabbed both tests and went inside Angel's bathroom to use them, and then we waited. The clock ticked so incredibly slow! Angel and I were so still that we could hear the little kids playing outside and the click of the second hand on her TLC wall clock I bought her for her birthday last year. It was the longest five minutes of my life. At 3:35, Angel jumped up and raced me to her bathroom counter. We bumped shoulders trying to squeeze through the doorway at the same time. "Ouch!" we both exclaimed simultaneously. I was too nervous so I let her look at the tests.

"What were the symbols again?" She demanded.

"Blue for positive and pink for negative. No symbols," I replied nervously. The lump in my throat and the butterflies in my stomach overwhelmed my body. Angel looked up at me after studying the sticks carefully.

CHAPTER TWENTY-NINE

"Obstacles"

"Does it stink like rotten meat?

Or crust and sugar over—

like a syrupy sweet?

Maybe it just sags

like a heavy load.

Or does it explode?"

From Harlem, by Langston Hughes

"Pink! Pink girlfriend! Pink!" She yelled in excitement. My knees were already weak, so they gave out instantly, and I fell to the floor with relief. After collecting myself, I reread both boxes to ensure that pink meant negative, and it did! I also saw my doctor a week later and didn't have any diseases. Angel went with me, of course, holding my hand the whole time.

I finally told Momma about my scare. She wasn't happy at all. She looked at me with still eyes. I thought I was going to turn to stone. Nothing in her room moved. The sheer white curtains stood at attention, ignoring the wind's command to move. The television commercial seemed to be in the same place when I entered the room. Her newly placed purse strap on the closet door knob stopped swinging, and I didn't dare blink until she did.

"Sit down, Moon," she demanded while clearing my father's work uniform out of the way and pushing back the blankets.

"Okay, Momma," I said calmly as I headed for the space designated for me right beside her.

"I want to share a story with you that I have not shared with anyone except those closest to me. Are you listening?" She inquired.

"Yes, Momma. I am," I replied attentively.

"Okay, good. About eighteen years ago, a young woman fell in love with a young man. He was not making the best of choices because he was only a boy himself and didn't know better yet. She didn't cause her mother any problems outside of the usual. She went to school, came home, did her homework, helped with daily chores, and kept to herself. She didn't realize that she was missing love. Don't misunderstand, Moon. Her mother loved her dearly, and she knew that, but because her mother was always busy working or caring for her siblings, she couldn't provide this young lady with the amount of love that she required, so the young woman clung to this young man. They were inseparable. When you saw one, you saw the other for four consecutive years. At the end of the fourth year, they both graduated from high school.

With this newfound time on his hands, the young man continued down the path of bad choices. A year went by, and the young lady started feeling like there was some sort of sickness growing inside of her that she didn't think was a big deal. She felt uncomfortable sometimes, but she never went to see a doctor or tell her mother. This discomfort she felt finally subsided, so the young lady didn't think about it again. The bad choices continued. She knew she should've left him but she didn't. Was that a good choice, Moon?"

"No, Momma," I replied, remaining attentive and wondering who these people were. She continued after sipping her tea and placing it neatly on the floral coaster on her nightstand.

"Six months later, she found out she was pregnant with her first child at the tender age of eighteen. She was pretty much a child herself. During the nine months that she carried her baby, the young man asked her to marry him. He got a job with the government and decided to turn away from those wild behaviors. However, Moon, there was no guarantee that he would turn his life around, so should she have left him when she found out about his poor choices," Momma primped her lips as she always did when she was disgusted about something.

"Yes, Momma. She should have," I stated more attentively.

"They got married while she was about three months pregnant against her mother's wishes and moved into a little one-bedroom apartment. Life seemed perfect. They were clearly not ready for this family they made, but they had no other choice but to make it work the best way they knew how, and they loved each other very much. Each day the young lady caught two buses to work. It was her first bookkeeping job. She started sitting in the seats with her legs facing parallel in the direction of the aisle because her stomach got too big to face the

seat in front of her. Every day, she went to work, and he went to work both barely earning enough to feed themselves and waiting for the day their little package would arrive. Eventually, one summer night, her water broke, and baby Hope arrived." She paused. I gasped in shock!

"Momma, that was you and Daddy?" I exclaimed.

"Yes, it was, baby, come closer to me," she commanded in a soft voice. I complied, laying my head on her lap.

"When I," Momma coughed with grief. She started crying and couldn't finish her sentence.

"Momma, it's okay. You don't have to finish the story," I said.

"Yes, I do, Moon," she declared. She grabbed a tissue from the box on her nightstand and blew her nose. She wiped the loose tears rolling down her cheeks. She continued. *"Moon, you were born legally blind because of all of that discomfort going on inside of me. I didn't realize that anything was wrong until it was too late. I did that to you, baby."*

I gasped again, but this time I jumped up. I couldn't even breathe. Tears started flowing like a stream flowing downward. I couldn't speak.

"Moon, baby, you okay?" For the first time since my sight was healed, I regretted having it. I didn't want to look at my mother. My legs got heavy, but somehow, I made it to my room and collapsed on my bed. I cried, and I cried, and I cried. I cried out of sympathy for myself. I cried out of empathy for my mother and father's innocence. I fell asleep in a puddle of tears.

CHAPTER THIRTY

"A Story To Tell"

"Through many dangers, toils and snares,
I have already come;
'Tis grace hath brought me safe thus far,
And grace will lead me home."
Amazing Grace by John Newton

I woke up the next morning with a lump of crust in my eyes and dried tears on my face. I thought it was all a dream until I realized I was wearing the same grey hoodie and cut-off jean shorts from yesterday. My journal was staring at me. Helen Keller was staring at me. I felt like she was telling me that just like her, I had a story to tell, one that could bring about change in the hearts and minds of people. I realized that my life at only seventeen was a compelling biography of faith, struggle, and triumph.

CHAPTER THIRTY-ONE

"My Written Story"

"You take up the pen when you are told, and write what is commanded.

There is no agony like bearing an untold story inside you."

Zora Neale Hurston

I sat down at my computer looking at a blank canvas. The cursor blinked at me as if asking me a question. I looked at it, started typing, and answered.

"MY STORY"

Prologue

I was born legally blind, so I see things, people, and beauty differently. I also believe that my disability makes me see things, ideas, mistakes, friendships, and love with appreciation. I appreciate the wall because it helped me learn boundaries and limitations early in my life. I'm thankful for the sun because it helped me see a little clearer as I awkwardly maneuvered my community. With clear vision today, as I admire its radiant light and ability to give life to so many things, including me, I realize its abundant power. I'm thankful for the people like the students in my first math class at DCU who led me to my desk and helped me situate my braille version of the textbook. I'm thankful for Angel's parents, who furnished their house in a strategic way just for me, and for mighty Ms. Maverick, who gave me the confidence I needed to exist as a blind young woman.

This world needs people like me who seek out the relevance of things big or small and attach them to a meaningful purpose. It is both the small and big that have brought me to where I am today. I don't know how long this experimental surgery is going to last. I may lose my sight tomorrow. I don't care. Sighted or unsighted, I can be and will be TRIUMPHANT!

"My Story"

Page One

I was born Alexandra Hope Neilson. My family and friends called me "Moon"...........

Epilogue

Through Her Eyes
By Major Craig Crowley U.S. Marine Corp.

It has often been said that real experience is the best teacher. Often, we reserve our ultimate respect for the soldier who has experienced deadly combat, the athlete who has won a hard-fought championship, and the single mother who has successfully raised a beautiful child. These heroes deserve our unreserved admiration because they have proven their value with relentless action and hard-won results. We want to be like them and imitate their lives to improve our own. Momma's stories were spellbinding for just that reason. She lived it, learned from it, and passed it on because she wanted to save us from our mistakes by removing the veil from our eyes! In doing so, she gave us Hope!

9 7 9 8 2 1 8 1 8 3 4 0 0